The Scholar's Game

The rules are written in shadow, and rebellion is the only way out.

Evelyn Harper

Copyright © 2024 by Evelyn Harper

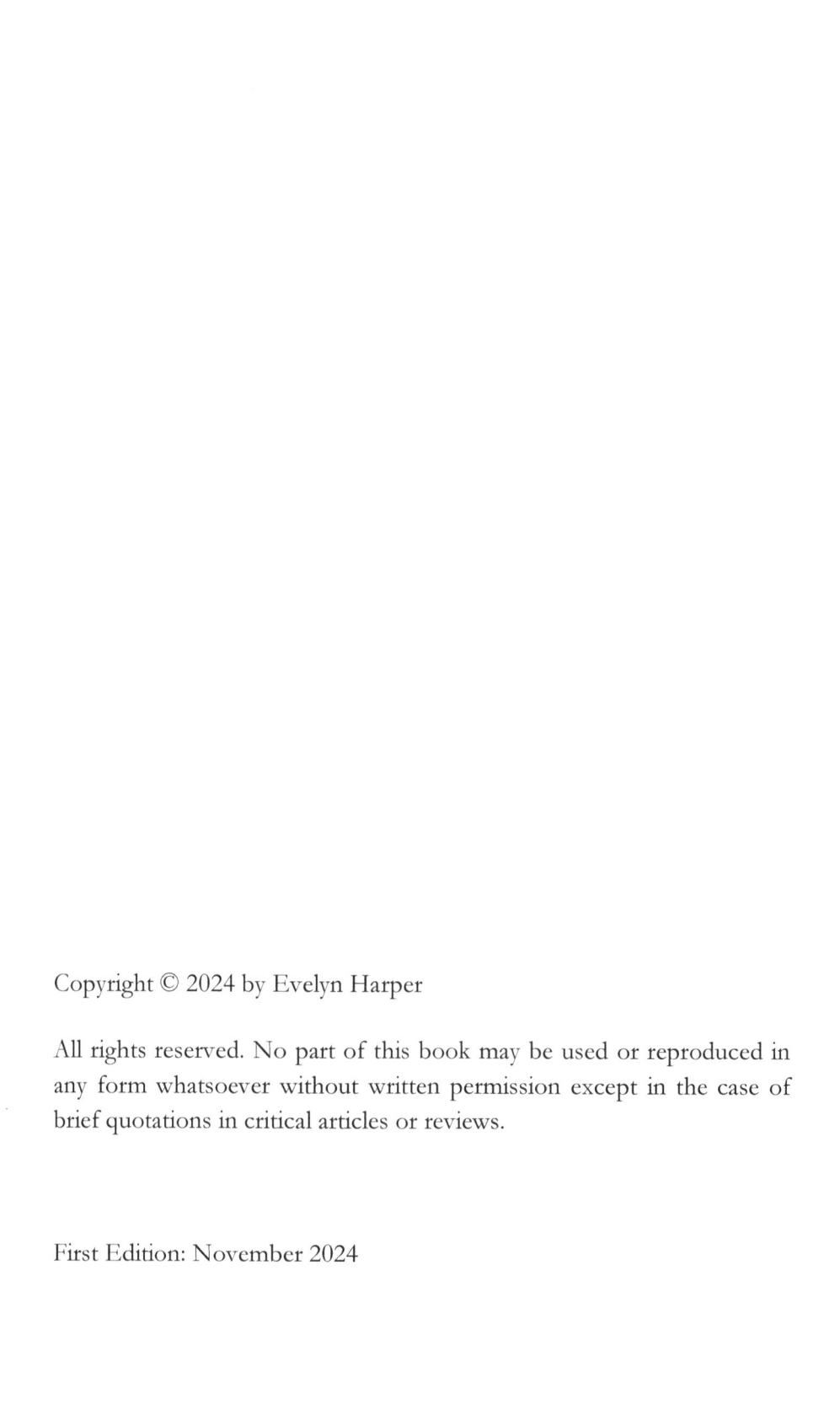

All rights reserved. No part of this book may be used or reproduced in any form whatsoever without written permission except in the case of brief quotations in critical articles or reviews.

First Edition: November 2024

Table of Contents

Chapter 1 The Gates of Barrington 1

Chapter 2 The Whispered Network 16

Chapter 3 Shadows of Control 32

Chapter 4 Silent Observers 49

Chapter 5 Warnings in the Dark 66

Chapter 6 The Price of Insight 82

Chapter 7 The Burden of Secrets 100

Chapter 8 Chains of Influence 117

Chapter 9 The Unseen Strings 133

Chapter 10 Testing the Boundaries 149

Chapter 11 Shattered Alliances 165

Chapter 12 Family Ties and False Truths 181

Chapter 13 Loyalty on Trial 196

Chapter 14 The Web Tightens 211

Chapter 15 The Crossroads of Conviction 227

Epilogue A Whisper of Freedom 243

Chapter 1
The Gates of Barrington

The bus screeched to a halt, its weathered brakes echoing through the stillness of Barrington College's front gates. Isabella Carter stepped out, her scuffed sneakers landing on the cobblestone path with a soft tap. Above her loomed an imposing arch, ivy draped across the gothic letters spelling "Barrington." The chill in the air pressed against her as if the campus itself wanted to size her up.

She pulled her duffle bag tighter to her side and tilted her head back, taking it all in. The grandeur of the place struck her like a punch. Towering spires pierced the gray sky, their intricate stonework twisting into gargoyle faces that seemed to leer at her. Ivy snaked across every wall, a living tapestry of history and privilege. She adjusted the strap of her bag, suddenly hyperaware of her thrift store jacket. Everything about this place screamed exclusivity, and here she was, a scholarship student from a town no one here would ever bother to visit.

"Move it, kid," a senior barked, shouldering past her with a confidence that could only be bred, not taught. She stepped aside hastily, her cheeks flushing as she fumbled with her bag. Around her, the quad bustled with students dragging their suitcases across the cobblestones, laughter bubbling in the crisp autumn air. Laughter she wasn't a part of.

Isabella's eyes darted to a group of girls lounging near the marble fountain at the center of the courtyard. Their effortless chatter filled the air, their designer boots crunching over fallen leaves like punctuation marks to a language Isabella didn't speak. She looked down at her own shoes and adjusted her glasses, suddenly conscious of how every detail about her screamed, **You don't belong here.**

A sharp whistle broke through her thoughts. Across the quad, a group of students congregated, their energy magnetic. At their center stood a tall figure with tousled dark hair and a quiet intensity that seemed to ripple outward. He leaned against a lamppost, a book tucked under his arm, the kind of detached cool that made it impossible not to look twice. Their eyes met for a fraction of a second. His gaze lingered, curious, before he returned to his book. Isabella's heart gave a disobedient flutter.

"Hey!" A chipper voice interrupted her trance. "You must be new."

Isabella turned to see a petite girl with bright pink hair and combat boots mismatched with her preppy sweater. "I'm Rachel. You look lost."

"I—uh, just got here," Isabella managed, feeling her Brooklyn accent claw its way into her words. She hated how it made her feel even more out of place.

Rachel tilted her head, studying her. "Scholarship?"

Isabella stiffened but nodded. It wasn't the first time she'd been read so easily.

"Relax," Rachel said, flashing a disarming grin. "Most of the scholarships end up in my dorm. Looks like you're stuck with me."

As Rachel led her toward the dorms, Isabella caught snippets of whispered conversations in the air.

"Did you hear? Another chosen scholar—"
"—the Syndicate must be watching her already—"
"—hope she knows what she signed up for—"

The words sent a shiver through Isabella, though she couldn't place why. A sense of something unseen crept into her thoughts, settling like an ache behind her ribs.

"Don't mind the whispers," Rachel said lightly. "This place thrives on drama. Just keep your head down, yeah?"

But Isabella couldn't shake the feeling that those whispers weren't idle gossip. They felt intentional. Purposeful. Like she'd just stepped into a game whose rules no one bothered to explain.

As they passed the Sundial Courtyard, Isabella glanced back. The boy with the book was gone, leaving only a swirl of fallen leaves in his place. For reasons she couldn't explain, her heart felt a little heavier as she followed Rachel toward the dorms, the whispers trailing behind her like ghosts.

The dormitory hummed with life. Laughter spilled into the halls as students leaned in doorways, swapping stories about summer trips to exclusive resorts and internships at their parents' firms. Every now and then, bursts of music erupted from an open room, blending with the rhythmic clamor of suitcases being dragged across the floor. Isabella paused at the threshold of her assigned dorm room, gripping her duffle bag tightly.

Inside, her roommate was already unpacked. A sleek, metallic suitcase sat propped open on the bed nearest the window, its contents carefully arranged: designer sweaters, meticulously folded jeans, and a toiletry kit that gleamed with labels Isabella only recognized from magazines.

Her roommate turned, her glossy hair flipping with a practiced ease. "Oh," she said, eyeing Isabella from head to toe. "You must be the other one. Isabella, right?"

"That's me," Isabella said, forcing a smile.

"I'm Penelope. Penny, actually," she said, stretching out a manicured hand. "Nice to meet you."

Isabella shook it, feeling the cool precision of Penny's grip.

"So, where are you from?" Penny asked, her tone polite but distracted as she adjusted a stack of books on her desk.

"Brooklyn," Isabella said.

Penny's perfectly arched eyebrows rose ever so slightly. "Oh, cool. I've been there. We usually stay at The Williamsburg Hotel when my dad has business in the city. Such a vibe."

"Right," Isabella said, unsure how to respond. She stepped further into the room, setting her duffle bag on the unclaimed bed. The mattress creaked under its weight, a sound that seemed to echo louder than it should have.

Penny didn't notice. "Anyway, I've got dinner plans with some friends tonight. Orientation stuff is pretty boring, but there's this party at the Theta House later. You should come! It's a great way to meet people."

"Maybe," Isabella said hesitantly.

Penny smiled brightly but didn't press. "Cool. Well, gotta run!" She grabbed her keys and a designer tote bag, her heels clicking against the polished floor as she left.

The door closed behind her, and Isabella was alone. She glanced around the room, taking in Penny's immaculate side with its coordinated bedding and soft, glowing fairy lights strung along the window. Her own bed, by contrast, looked stark and uninviting.

She sighed, pulling out her sheets and tossing them onto the mattress. As she worked, voices from the hallway seeped through the thin walls.

"God, I haven't seen you since Aspen!" "Let's get brunch tomorrow; my treat." "Can you believe the new scholarship kids? They look so… overwhelmed."

Isabella froze at the last comment, her hands clutching a pillowcase. The voices faded, replaced by the sound of muffled laughter, but the sting lingered.

Later, she wandered the campus alone, her hands stuffed into the pockets of her jacket. The quad had transformed into a tableau of reunions, old friends embracing and new alliances forming over cups of coffee from the campus café.

She found a bench near the edge of the quad, just outside the reach of a flickering streetlamp. From there, she watched the scene unfold, her chest tightening with each passing moment.

"Mind if I sit?" a voice asked, pulling her out of her thoughts.

Isabella looked up to see Rachel, her pink hair now tied back into a messy bun, balancing two steaming cups of coffee. "Figured you could use this," Rachel said, handing her one.

"Thanks," Isabella murmured, wrapping her hands around the warm cup.

Rachel plopped down beside her. "Rough start?"

"Something like that," Isabella admitted. "Everyone seems to already know each other. Or at least know how to belong here."

Rachel snorted. "Yeah, well, that's the charm of Barrington. You either fit the mold or spend your time pretending you do." She sipped her coffee, her gaze fixed on the group nearest the fountain. "Let me guess: your roommate's already invited you to some exclusive party?"

"Something like that," Isabella said, a wry smile tugging at her lips.

Rachel leaned closer, lowering her voice conspiratorially. "Pro tip? Skip it. Those parties are just an excuse for the rich kids to compare trust funds."

Isabella laughed softly. "Noted."

For a moment, the two sat in companionable silence, the hum of the campus fading into the background.

"You'll find your rhythm here," Rachel said eventually. "It just takes time. And maybe a thick skin."

Isabella nodded, grateful for the reassurance but still feeling the weight of her isolation. She took a sip of her coffee, the warmth spreading through her chest.

"By the way," Rachel added, standing up. "There's more to this place than meets the eye. If you stick around long enough, you'll see what I mean."

Before Isabella could ask what she meant, Rachel had already disappeared into the crowd, leaving her alone again.

She leaned back on the bench, staring up at the spires silhouetted against the night sky. A sense of unease prickled at the edge of her thoughts. She didn't know what Rachel meant, but she had a feeling she was about to find out.

Isabella wandered aimlessly across the quad, the late afternoon light slanting golden across the ivy-clad walls. Her mind churned with the events of the day, the endless stream of faces, the clipped conversations that carried undertones of judgment and expectation. She didn't belong here—not really. The thought settled heavily in her chest as she meandered toward the fountain at the center of the courtyard, its trickling water oddly soothing against the backdrop of animated chatter.

She perched on the edge of the stone rim, adjusting her glasses and hugging her arms around her knees. Groups of students milled about in every direction, their laughter cutting through the crisp autumn air. Isabella watched them with a detached curiosity, her gaze flitting from one cluster to the next. She could already see the social hierarchies forming, as though they had arrived preordained.

Her thoughts broke when she noticed him.

He was leaning against a weathered lamppost just beyond the fountain, his figure partially obscured by the dappled shadows of a sprawling oak. Tall and broad-shouldered, he carried himself with a quiet intensity that set him apart from the surrounding bustle. His dark hair caught the sunlight in muted streaks, and his posture—relaxed but somehow vigilant—suggested a depth that piqued her interest.

Isabella tried to look away, but her gaze lingered. He was reading a book, one hand holding the spine open while the other rested casually in the pocket of his jacket. Something about him seemed... untouchable. He didn't laugh or gesture like the other students. Instead, he seemed to exist on the edge of the moment, a world unto himself.

And then he looked up.

Their eyes met, and the air between them shifted.

Isabella froze, caught in the gravity of his gaze. It wasn't just the color of his eyes—a stormy gray that seemed to catch the light—but the way he looked at her, as if seeing something he hadn't expected. His expression was unreadable, a blend of curiosity and something sharper, something that sent a faint shiver down her spine.

She blinked and broke the connection, her heart thudding painfully against her ribs. She felt ridiculous. He was just another student, probably a senior with more important things to think about than the awkward scholarship girl gawking at him from across the quad.

She reached for her bag, fumbling for her notebook as a distraction.

"You okay?" a voice asked, startling her.

Isabella glanced up to see Rachel, her pink-haired guide from earlier, approaching with an amused smirk.

"Fine," Isabella said quickly. She tucked her notebook against her chest, as if it could shield her from whatever judgment Rachel might be forming.

Rachel followed her line of sight and grinned. "Ohhh, I see."

"What?" Isabella said, a little too quickly.

"Don't play coy," Rachel teased, plopping down beside her. "You've got your eyes on the mysterious senior."

"I don't know what you're talking about," Isabella muttered, though her cheeks betrayed her with a sudden warmth.

Rachel laughed. "That's Benjamin Foster. Ben. Total enigma, if you ask me. Keeps to himself most of the time, but when he talks? People listen. It's kind of his thing."

"Why?" Isabella asked, unable to suppress her curiosity.

Rachel shrugged. "Probably because he's brilliant. Or maybe it's the broody vibe. I'm not sure which." She nudged Isabella lightly. "But word to the wise? Don't get too attached to the idea of him. Guys like that come with baggage. Heavy, mysterious baggage."

"I wasn't—" Isabella began, but Rachel cut her off.

"Sure, you weren't." Rachel's smirk widened. "But if you're curious, he's big on philosophy. You'd probably get along."

Isabella rolled her eyes but couldn't help sneaking another glance toward the lamppost. Ben was gone, his book left leaning against the base of the post.

"Come on," Rachel said, standing and stretching. "Dinner's calling, and you look like you could use a real meal."

Isabella followed her reluctantly, her mind still on the boy with the book and the eyes that had looked right through her.

As they walked away, she couldn't resist asking, "What's his deal?"

Rachel grinned knowingly. "That's the million-dollar question, isn't it? Stick around long enough, and you might find out."

The answer didn't satisfy her, but Isabella let it drop. Even as the noise of the dining hall enveloped her later, she couldn't shake the feeling that Ben Foster had seen something in her that she didn't yet understand. Or maybe it was just her imagination.

Either way, her pulse quickened at the thought of him, a boy who seemed to carry the weight of secrets too heavy to share.

The grand lecture hall was packed, its cavernous walls humming with the energy of nearly a hundred first-year students. Isabella sat near the back, her notebook open but untouched as the orientation speaker—a dean with a commanding voice and a penchant for overly dramatic pauses—droned on about academic excellence and the "prestigious legacy of Barrington College."

The chandeliers overhead flickered slightly, casting shifting shadows across the rows of students. Isabella leaned back in her chair, her gaze wandering over the sea of faces. Most of them looked as though they belonged here—bright-eyed, eager, wearing confidence like an accessory. She felt more like an outsider than ever, clutching her pen like a lifeline.

"—our chosen scholars represent the very best of what Barrington stands for," the dean was saying, his voice rising to emphasize the words.

Isabella sat up straighter. Chosen scholars?

The phrase hung in the air for a moment before the dean moved on, but her curiosity was piqued. She scribbled the term in the margin of her notebook, circling it twice.

"Did you hear that?" a girl nearby whispered to her friend, her voice low but sharp.

"Yeah," the friend replied, her tone a mix of awe and apprehension. "They say the chosen ones get... special attention."

Isabella pretended to adjust her glasses, tilting her head slightly to catch more of their conversation.

"Special attention, like what?" the first girl asked.

"Like… they're groomed for something," the friend said, her voice barely audible now. "My brother's friend was one last year. He said it's not just about academics. It's—"

"Shh!" The first girl cut her off, her eyes darting toward the front of the room where a proctor was scanning the rows.

Isabella's pulse quickened. She glanced down at her notebook again, the words "chosen scholars" glaring back at her like an accusation.

"What does that even mean?" she muttered under her breath.

The girl sitting next to her, a sharp-featured blonde with an air of perpetual disinterest, must have heard. She turned slightly, raising an eyebrow. "You don't know about the chosen scholars?"

Isabella blinked. "No. Should I?"

The girl smirked faintly, as if deciding whether to indulge her. "It's just a rumor. You know, elite group, secret perks, that kind of thing. Probably just a way to freak out the new kids."

"Right," Isabella said, though her unease didn't fade.

As the session dragged on, she couldn't help but glance around the room, wondering if anyone here knew more. The dean's words had felt deliberate, almost like a challenge. Was it just standard orientation hype, or was there something more to it?

When the lecture finally ended, Isabella shuffled out with the crowd, her notebook clutched tightly in her hand. The quad was bathed in the soft glow of early evening, the gothic spires of the campus casting long shadows across the cobblestones.

She found Rachel waiting for her by the fountain, a half-eaten granola bar in hand.

"Hey, how was orientation?" Rachel asked, chewing noisily.

"Fine," Isabella said distractedly. "Weird, though. Do you know anything about… chosen scholars?"

Rachel froze mid-bite, her expression carefully neutral. "Where'd you hear that?"

"The dean mentioned it," Isabella said, watching her closely. "And some people were talking about it. It sounded… strange."

Rachel swallowed hard and forced a laugh. "Oh, that. Yeah, it's just Barrington lore. Every college has its urban legends, right? Don't let it get to you."

"You don't think it's real?" Isabella pressed.

"Honestly?" Rachel hesitated, then shrugged. "I think it's just a story to make the rest of us feel like peasants. You know, keep the mystique alive."

But Isabella wasn't convinced. Rachel's nonchalance felt practiced, like she was skirting around something.

"Anyway," Rachel added, tossing the granola wrapper into her bag. "You should come to the library later. It's quieter than the dorms, and you can get a head start on your reading. Plus, the place is stunning. Might take your mind off the whole… chosen thing."

Isabella nodded, though her thoughts were still tangled. "Sure. Thanks."

As Rachel led her toward the library, Isabella glanced over her shoulder. The campus seemed darker now, the cheerful chatter of students muted against the low rustle of the wind.

Chosen scholars. Special attention. Groomed for something.

The words looped through her mind, leaving a chill in their wake. Whatever the truth was, she had the unsettling feeling that she wasn't meant to know it. Not yet.

Chapter 2
The Whispered Network

The sunlight streamed through the tall windows of Hawthorne Hall, painting the lecture room in warm, golden hues. Isabella shifted in her seat, her notebook open and ready, her pen poised above the first blank page. Around her, students leaned back casually, their conversations an easy blend of confidence and familiarity. For Isabella, this was the moment she'd been waiting for: her first class at Barrington College.

"Welcome to Modern Philosophy," the professor began, his voice a deep, melodic cadence that commanded attention. "This course is not about memorizing facts. It's about questioning the world, questioning yourselves, and embracing the uncomfortable ambiguity of truth."

Isabella's pen flew across the page, capturing every word. The pace of the lecture was brisk, the ideas complex and intoxicating. She felt a surge of exhilaration; this was the reason she'd worked so hard to get here.

The professor continued, weaving ideas from Descartes to Nietzsche, and for a moment, Isabella forgot about her earlier anxieties. The thrill of learning, of immersing herself in this world of intellect and possibility, was everything she'd dreamed of.

As the lecture wound down, Isabella sat back, her notebook filled with scribbled notes and questions. The professor dismissed the class with a wave of his hand. "Remember, the purpose of philosophy is not to find answers but to understand the questions. See you Wednesday."

Students began filing out, their voices blending into a low hum. Isabella lingered, wanting to soak in the moment a little longer.

"Not bad for a first class, huh?" a familiar voice said behind her.

She turned to see Rachel, her ever-relaxed pink-haired guide, grinning as she slung her bag over one shoulder.

"Not bad at all," Isabella agreed, her smile breaking through unbidden.

Rachel leaned closer. "Careful, though. Professors here love throwing curveballs. You'll be knee-deep in papers before you know it."

"I can handle it," Isabella said, a mix of confidence and determination lacing her tone.

"I like the spirit," Rachel said with a smirk. "Come on, lunch awaits. You'll need fuel for the next round of brain-melting lectures."

As they exited the building, Isabella couldn't help but notice something odd. A chandelier in the hallway, its intricate design wrought in twisting iron, glinted with what looked like tiny, embedded lenses. Her steps faltered.

"What's up?" Rachel asked, pausing beside her.

"That chandelier…" Isabella pointed. "It has cameras in it."

Rachel glanced at it, her expression unreadable. "Yeah, this place loves its surveillance. Keeps everyone on their best behavior, I guess."

"Isn't that… weird?" Isabella asked, frowning.

Rachel shrugged. "You're at Barrington. Nothing here is normal. Just wait until you see the library."

The cryptic remark left Isabella uneasy, but she let Rachel lead her toward the dining hall. By late afternoon, Isabella found herself in her second class of the day, Advanced Literary Analysis. The room was smaller, the discussion more intimate. This time, the professor paced the length of the classroom, gesturing animatedly as he spoke about symbolism and the weight of language.

Isabella quickly fell into the rhythm, her thoughts dancing with possibilities as the class explored the interplay of text and meaning. But as she reached for her pen to jot down an idea, her eyes caught another strange detail: a polished wooden clock on the far wall, its face adorned with delicate carvings. It was beautiful, but something about it felt… off.

When the class ended, Isabella lingered again, her curiosity pulling her closer to the clock.

"You're going to be late for your next class if you keep that up," said a low, amused voice.

She turned sharply to see Ben Foster leaning casually against the doorframe, his arms crossed.

"Do you always sneak up on people?" Isabella asked, trying to mask her surprise.

He smirked, his storm-gray eyes flicking toward the clock. "Not sneaking. Just observing. It's a habit."

Isabella glanced back at the clock. "What's with these things? The chandeliers, the clocks... It feels like someone's watching."

Ben's smirk faded, replaced by something more serious. "They probably are."

Her stomach twisted at his words. "What does that mean?"

Ben straightened, stepping into the room. "It means you're at Barrington, and Barrington has rules. Some of them you'll learn. Others... you'll wish you hadn't."

She narrowed her eyes at him. "You're being cryptic on purpose."

"Maybe." His tone was light, but his gaze was sharp, studying her as if weighing how much to say.

"Care to elaborate?" she pressed.

Ben hesitated for a fraction of a second, then shook his head. "Not here. Not now." He started to walk away, then paused at the doorway. "Keep your head down, Isabella. And maybe don't stare at the clocks."

Before she could respond, he was gone, leaving her alone with the unsettling hum of the room. Isabella stared at the clock for a moment longer, the intricacy of its design suddenly feeling suffocating. She turned and hurried out, the thrill of her classes now tinged with an unshakable sense of unease.

Isabella smoothed her sweater nervously as she stood outside Professor Thorne's office. The door, an imposing slab of dark wood adorned with a polished brass nameplate, seemed to stare back at her, daring her to knock. She hesitated, replaying the words from the email she'd received that morning: **"Isabella, I'd like to discuss your scholarship and future opportunities at Barrington. Please see me during office hours today."**

The email hadn't specified a reason, but there was something about its tone—formal, yet faintly suggestive—that unsettled her. Taking a deep breath, she knocked twice.

"Come in," a voice called, smooth and precise.

She pushed the door open to find Professor Elias Thorne seated behind a massive desk, its surface meticulously organized with leather-bound books, a vintage clock, and a single fountain pen. The office smelled faintly of old paper and cedarwood, the warm light from a desk lamp casting sharp shadows.

"Miss Carter," Thorne said, standing and gesturing toward a chair across from him. "Please, have a seat."

"Thank you," Isabella murmured, stepping forward and sitting carefully, her hands folded in her lap.

Thorne studied her for a moment, his sharp eyes framed by wire-rimmed glasses. He was younger than she'd expected, his dark hair streaked with only the faintest trace of gray. His demeanor exuded a controlled confidence that made the room feel smaller.

"I've been reviewing your file," Thorne began, leaning back in his chair. "Your academic record is exceptional. Top marks in every subject, glowing recommendations. It's no surprise you were awarded the Barrington Foundation Scholarship."

"Thank you," Isabella said, though her voice felt small.

Thorne tilted his head, his gaze unrelenting. "How are you finding Barrington so far?"

"It's... a lot," she admitted. "The classes are challenging, which I like. But the rest of it—fitting in—it's been an adjustment."

"Ah, yes," Thorne said with a knowing smile. "The social dynamics here can be... daunting, especially for someone without certain advantages."

Isabella's cheeks flushed. "I'm just trying to focus on why I'm here."

"An admirable approach," Thorne said, nodding approvingly. "And precisely why I wanted to speak with you. You see, Miss Carter, Barrington is not merely an institution for higher learning. It is a crucible—a place where the brightest minds are forged into something greater."

His words hung in the air, heavy with implication. Isabella leaned forward slightly, unable to suppress her curiosity. "What do you mean?"

Thorne's lips curled into a faint smile. "Your scholarship places you among an elite group of students. These individuals—chosen not just for their intellect but for their potential—are given opportunities to transcend the ordinary paths of academia. To make a true impact."

"Opportunities?" Isabella echoed, her pulse quickening.

"Indeed," Thorne said, steepling his fingers. "But such opportunities are not handed out indiscriminately. They are earned through dedication, ambition, and a willingness to go beyond what is expected."

Isabella hesitated, her mind racing. "Go beyond in what way?"

Thorne leaned forward, his tone growing more intimate. "It means embracing challenges that others might shy away from. Taking risks. Demonstrating not just intelligence, but resolve."

The room felt suddenly warmer, the air heavy with unspoken meaning. Isabella's heart thudded in her chest. "I don't understand. Are you talking about extracurriculars? Research projects?"

Thorne chuckled softly, though the sound carried little humor. "In a manner of speaking. You'll find, Miss Carter, that the most rewarding paths at Barrington are often the least conventional. But those paths are not for everyone."

"Why not?" she asked, her voice sharper now.

Thorne's gaze darkened, his smile thinning. "Because not everyone has the fortitude to walk them. And that is not a criticism—it is simply reality."

Isabella swallowed hard, unsure whether she was being complimented or tested. "Are you saying I do?"

Thorne studied her for a moment before nodding slowly. "I believe you might. But potential, Miss Carter, is only the beginning. It is what you choose to do with it that defines you."

His words sent a shiver down her spine. "I'm willing to work hard. Always have been."

"Good," Thorne said, his smile returning. "Then let this be the start of a... deeper conversation. I'll be watching your progress with great interest."

As he rose to signal the end of the meeting, Isabella stood as well, clutching her bag tightly. "Thank you, Professor Thorne," she said, her voice steady despite the unease coiling in her stomach.

"Think nothing of it," Thorne replied, extending a hand. "And remember, Miss Carter: the paths less traveled often lead to the most extraordinary destinations. But only if one is prepared to pay the price."

Isabella shook his hand, her palm clammy against his firm grip. As she stepped into the hallway, the door closing softly behind her, his words echoed in her mind. **The most extraordinary destinations… but only if one is prepared to pay the price.**

Her steps quickened, the faintest flicker of dread sparking in her chest. Whatever this "opportunity" was, she had the unsettling feeling that it came with strings attached—strings she might not want to untangle.

The fading sunlight cast long shadows over the cobblestones as Isabella trudged back toward her dorm. Professor Thorne's words echoed in her mind, their deliberate phrasing nagging at her like a splinter beneath the skin. There had been something in his tone, something careful but weighted. She couldn't quite put her finger on it, but it left her uneasy.

The soft crunch of footsteps behind her broke her reverie. She glanced over her shoulder and saw Ben Foster matching her pace, hands tucked into the pockets of his coat.

"You following me now?" Isabella asked, her tone light but edged with curiosity.

Ben smirked faintly. "Not following. Just heading the same way."

"Convenient," she said, adjusting the strap of her bag.

They walked in silence for a moment before Ben spoke again. "So, what did Thorne want?"

Isabella frowned, glancing at him. "How did you know I met with him?"

"Everyone who's on a scholarship ends up in his orbit eventually," Ben replied, his voice low. "It's part of the deal."

"The deal?" she echoed, her chest tightening.

Ben stopped, turning to face her. "Look, Thorne's not just a professor. He's... involved. Think of him as a gatekeeper. He decides who gets in and who stays out."

"Gets into what?" Isabella pressed, her voice rising slightly.

Ben's jaw tightened, and he looked away, scanning the path ahead as if searching for eavesdroppers. "It's not something we talk about in the open."

She crossed her arms, frustration bubbling to the surface. "You realize how shady that sounds, right?"

"Good," Ben said, his gray eyes locking onto hers with an intensity that made her breath hitch. "You should think it's shady. Because it is."

Isabella hesitated, trying to read his expression. "If you're trying to scare me, it's working."

"I'm not trying to scare you," he said, his tone softening. "I'm trying to warn you."

"Warn me about what?" she asked, her voice quieter now.

Ben sighed, rubbing the back of his neck. "The scholarship isn't free, Isabella. There are expectations. Obligations. And Thorne is the one who enforces them."

Her stomach dropped. "Obligations? Like what? He didn't say anything about that when I met with him."

"He wouldn't," Ben said with a bitter laugh. "Not at first. They ease you in. Little tasks, things that seem harmless. But before you know it, you're in too deep to back out."

She stared at him, her mind racing. "Why are you telling me this?"

"Because you seem like someone who still has a choice," he said, his voice barely above a whisper. "Most people don't realize what they're getting into until it's too late."

Isabella shook her head, trying to process his words. "This can't be real. You're making it sound like some kind of secret society or something."

Ben's expression didn't waver. "Call it whatever you want. But just know that once you're in, they don't let you go easily."

A chill ran down her spine. "Are you... in?"

His silence was answer enough. He looked away, his jaw tightening again. "Let's just say I know how it works."

She exhaled shakily, her breath visible in the cool evening air. "What do I do?"

"For now? Keep your head down," Ben said, his tone firm. "Don't ask too many questions. Don't draw too much attention. And definitely don't trust anyone who seems too eager to help."

"That's not exactly reassuring," Isabella muttered.

"It's not supposed to be," he said with a faint smirk. "Just stay sharp. You're smart—you'll figure it out."

She looked at him, searching for any sign of reassurance, but all she found was the same guarded intensity that had unsettled her since the moment she'd met him.

"Thanks, I guess," she said finally, her voice tinged with both gratitude and uncertainty.

Ben gave her a small nod. "See you around, Isabella."

He turned and walked away, his silhouette disappearing into the growing darkness. Isabella stood there for a moment, her heart pounding in her chest.

Thorne's words, Ben's warning—it all swirled together in her mind, forming a storm of suspicion and dread. She tightened her grip on her bag and quickened her pace, eager to reach the relative safety of her dorm.

As she climbed the steps to her building, she glanced over her shoulder one last time, half-expecting to see someone watching her. The path behind her was empty, but the feeling of unease lingered, heavier than ever.

The Fiske Library was a maze of shadowy alcoves and towering shelves, its ancient wooden floors creaking softly underfoot. Isabella tucked herself into a corner on the second floor, her books and notes spread out in front of her. The soft glow of a desk lamp illuminated the pages as she scribbled furiously, trying to make sense of the dense philosophical text.

Every so often, she paused, glancing up at the quiet grandeur of the library. There was something almost reverent about the space, as if it demanded a certain kind of respect. Yet the quiet wasn't soothing. It was heavy, charged, as though the walls themselves carried secrets.

A shadow flickered in the corner of her eye. She looked up sharply, her heart skipping a beat.

Ben Foster stood a few feet away, leaning casually against a nearby shelf. His storm-gray eyes met hers, a faint smirk playing on his lips.

"You've got the focused look down," he said. "That's a good start."

Isabella frowned, her pen still poised mid-air. "Were you watching me?"

"Just passing by," Ben said, his tone light but his gaze unreadable. "You're new. I was curious."

Her brow furrowed as she set her pen down. "Curious about what?"

He stepped closer, his movements unhurried. "About how long it'll take before you start asking the real questions."

Isabella's stomach twisted. "What's that supposed to mean?"

Ben shrugged, sliding his hands into his pockets. "It means Barrington's not just a college, Isabella. It's... layered."

"Layered?" she echoed, her frustration bubbling to the surface. "Do you always talk in riddles, or is that just for me?"

Ben chuckled softly, but the sound didn't reach his eyes. "I'm trying to help you."

"Help me how?" she pressed, standing now, her notebook forgotten. "By being cryptic? By acting like you know something I don't?"

His smirk faded, replaced by a seriousness that sent a chill down her spine. "I do know something you don't. And I'm telling you: careful who you trust here."

Her heart thudded painfully against her ribs. "Is this about Professor Thorne? About the scholarship?"

Ben tilted his head, studying her. "What did he say to you?"

"Nothing specific," she admitted, crossing her arms. "Just a lot of talk about 'opportunities' and potential. But it felt... off."

Ben's expression darkened. "It should. Thorne doesn't just 'mentor' scholarship students. He grooms them."

"Grooms them for what?" Isabella demanded, her voice rising despite the quiet of the library.

Ben took a step closer, his voice dropping to a near whisper. "For a game you don't want to play."

The weight of his words hung between them, suffocating. Isabella's throat felt tight. "Why are you telling me this?"

"Because you still have a choice," he said, his tone laced with something that almost sounded like regret.

"Do you?" she asked, her voice softer now.

Ben's jaw tightened, and for a moment, his carefully crafted exterior cracked. "Not anymore."

The raw honesty in his eyes startled her. "Then help me," she said, her voice almost a plea.

His gaze shifted, scanning the surrounding shelves before returning to her. "I already am," he said quietly. Then, before she could respond, he turned and strode down the aisle, disappearing into the maze of bookshelves.

Isabella stood frozen, her thoughts spinning wildly. She sank back into her chair, her hands trembling as she picked up her pen.

The words on the page blurred, her mind too clouded to focus. Ben's warning repeated in her head like a mantra: **Careful who you trust.**

But as she sat there, the library's oppressive silence pressing in on her, a darker question began to take shape.

Who could she trust at all?

Chapter 3
Shadows of Control

Isabella tucked herself into the farthest corner of the Barrington library, a fortress of silence surrounded by towering shelves of books. She adjusted her glasses and bent over her notebook, pretending to study as a low hum of conversation drifted toward her. Most students adhered to the unspoken rule of quiet in the library, but this was different—quick, hushed voices carried a tone of urgency, as though the speakers weren't just chatting but conspiring.

"She's one of them," a voice hissed, barely audible above the scratch of pens on paper. "A chosen scholar."

Isabella's ears pricked up. She tilted her head ever so slightly, catching sight of two students huddled over a table a few rows away. Their body language was stiff, their heads close together as if they feared being overheard.

"You can't be sure," the second student muttered, her voice tinged with uncertainty.

"I am. I saw her schedule, the professors she's meeting with. She fits the pattern."

The first student's words were quick, sharp. "You don't get into those meetings unless they've already decided. You know that. And you know what it means."

Isabella frowned, her pen hovering above the notebook. The words didn't make sense, but the tone did. It was the same guarded tone people used when they talked about things they didn't want others to know they knew.

"What if they're wrong?" the second voice whispered.

"They're never wrong," came the reply, this time with a note of finality.

The second student shifted in her seat, and her chair squeaked faintly. "Do you think she knows? About… about them?"

Isabella's chest tightened. Them. The word hung in the air like a warning, heavy and unspoken.

The first student scoffed. "They never tell the chosen ones, not at first. But they're watching her. Always. Just like they watch all of us."

A shiver ran down Isabella's spine. She wasn't sure what unsettled her more—the idea of someone watching or the resigned certainty in the speaker's voice. She leaned forward, her gaze flicking between the pages of her notebook and the two students, hoping they wouldn't notice her.

"They're probably watching us right now," the second student said, her voice trembling.

"Then keep your voice down," the first one snapped.

A new voice broke through the tension.

"Ladies," a calm, measured tone called out from the shadows of the nearby bookshelf.

Isabella's head snapped up. A tall, lean figure emerged from the shadows, his expression as still and precise as his tone. Professor Andrews, one of the younger faculty members, stepped forward, his hands clasped behind his back. His eyes flicked between the two students, and they froze, their faces drained of color.

"Is there a reason your discussion needs to happen here?" Andrews asked, his voice pleasant yet sharp.

The first student swallowed hard. "No, sir. We were just—"

"Studying, I'm sure," Andrews interrupted, his tone growing colder. "But I suggest you relocate your... study group to a more appropriate venue. Or perhaps focus on the task at hand."

The second student nodded rapidly, grabbing her books and shoving them into her bag. "Yes, Professor. Of course."

The first student muttered something under her breath as they scrambled to leave, their movements clumsy and rushed. Andrews watched them go, his expression unreadable, before turning his attention to the rest of the library. His gaze swept the room like a searchlight, pausing only briefly when it passed over Isabella.

Her breath caught, but she forced herself to look down, feigning disinterest.

"Carry on," Andrews said, his voice directed at no one in particular. He turned and strode toward the exit, his footsteps soft but deliberate.

The library fell silent once more, but the air felt heavier, thicker. Isabella's pen trembled in her hand as she tried to refocus on her notes.

Chosen scholars. Watching. Them.

The words looped in her mind, each one sharp and distinct, like shards of glass. She glanced toward the now-empty table where the two students had been sitting, her thoughts racing.

Who were "they," and why did the professor seem so determined to stop the conversation?

For the first time since she'd arrived at Barrington, Isabella felt a creeping sense of dread. This wasn't just an exclusive school with quirky traditions and high expectations. There was something else here, something larger, darker.

And whatever it was, she was certain it had noticed her.

The air in the quad was crisp with the scent of autumn, leaves swirling in lazy spirals around the cobblestones. Isabella walked with her hands stuffed deep into her jacket pockets, her mind spinning with fragments of the whispered conversation she'd overheard in the library. "Chosen scholars." "They're watching." The words wouldn't stop echoing in her head.

"Hey, earth to Isabella!" Rachel's bright, almost sing-song voice cut through the haze.

Isabella startled, nearly tripping over her own feet. Rachel grinned at her, falling into step beside her with a practiced ease.

"You looked like you were about to solve the mysteries of the universe," Rachel teased, her pink hair catching the sunlight as she nudged Isabella lightly with her elbow.

"Just… thinking," Isabella muttered, her voice distant.

Rachel raised an eyebrow. "Thinking, huh? Dangerous habit around here."

Isabella hesitated, her gaze flicking around the quad as if expecting someone to emerge from the shadows. "Rachel, can I ask you something?"

"You just did," Rachel quipped, though her grin softened when she noticed Isabella's serious expression. "Okay, shoot. What's up?"

Isabella glanced around again, lowering her voice. "What do you know about… chosen scholars?"

Rachel's easy smile faltered, replaced by a flicker of something sharp and wary. "Why are you asking that?"

"Because—" Isabella hesitated, debating whether to share what she'd overheard. She settled on a half-truth. "Someone mentioned it in the library. It sounded… strange."

Rachel sighed, running a hand through her pink hair and looking away. "Let me guess. They were whispering like the walls had ears?"

"Pretty much," Isabella admitted.

"They're not wrong," Rachel muttered under her breath. Her tone was light, but there was a tension beneath it that made Isabella's stomach tighten.

"What's that supposed to mean?" Isabella pressed, stepping in front of Rachel to block her path.

Rachel stopped, her expression hardening as she crossed her arms. "It means, Barrington has a lot of quirks. And not all of them are harmless."

"Like what?" Isabella asked, her voice edged with frustration. "Why can't anyone just give me a straight answer?"

Rachel glanced around the quad, scanning for eavesdroppers before leaning in closer. "Look, Isabella, there are things about this place that are better left alone. The less you know, the safer you'll be."

"That's not an answer," Isabella shot back. "If there's something I should be worried about, don't you think I deserve to know?"

Rachel's gaze softened, but her tone remained firm. "I'm telling you the truth. Just... don't draw attention to yourself, okay?

Don't ask too many questions, don't stand out, and for the love of all that's holy, don't get too curious about the wrong things."

Isabella frowned, frustration bubbling under her skin. "So, what? I'm just supposed to keep my head down and pretend nothing's happening?"

Rachel shrugged, her lips pressing into a thin line. "It's worked for me so far."

"That's not exactly comforting," Isabella muttered.

"It's not supposed to be," Rachel replied, her voice softening. "Listen, I like you, Isabella. You're smart, and you're... different. But that's exactly why you have to be careful. People like you, you get noticed."

"Noticed by who?" Isabella demanded.

Rachel hesitated, her jaw tightening. For a moment, it looked like she might actually answer, but then she shook her head. "It doesn't matter. Just trust me on this. Keep your head down, do your work, and don't give anyone a reason to look too closely at you."

Isabella opened her mouth to argue, but Rachel held up a hand to stop her.

"I'm serious," Rachel said, her tone uncharacteristically grave. "You think you're just here to study, to get your fancy degree and go back to wherever you came from? This place doesn't work like that. Barrington... it changes people. It tests them."

"Tests them how?" Isabella asked, her voice barely above a whisper.

Rachel shook her head again, stepping past Isabella and resuming her walk toward the dorms. "You don't want to know."

Isabella stood frozen for a moment, watching Rachel's retreating figure. Her mind raced with questions, each one more urgent than the last. She clenched her fists, frustration mingling with fear.

"Hey!" she called after Rachel, jogging to catch up. "If you're so worried about me, why not just tell me the truth?"

Rachel stopped again, turning slowly to face her. Her expression was unreadable, but her eyes were filled with something Isabella couldn't quite place—fear? Pity?

"Because the truth isn't going to help you," Rachel said quietly. "It's just going to make you a target."

With that, she turned and walked away, leaving Isabella alone in the swirling leaves of the quad. Isabella's heart pounded in her chest, her unease deepening with every step Rachel took away from her.

Keep your head down. Don't ask questions. Don't stand out.

But how could she, when it felt like the entire campus was built on secrets waiting to be uncovered?

Isabella lingered in the grand dining hall, her eyes tracing the intricate patterns carved into the gothic arches that framed the massive space. Afternoon light poured through stained-glass windows, casting colorful patches across the polished wooden floor. It was a scene out of a storybook, yet something about it felt unsettling.

Her gaze drifted upward to the chandeliers—great, sprawling pieces of wrought iron and glass that hung like guardians over the room. One, in particular, caught her attention.

At first, it was just an idle observation. The chandelier nearest the center of the hall gleamed faintly, its curved arms twisting like vines. But as she looked closer, she noticed a pattern embedded within the design—a crest, subtle but deliberate, etched into the iron at the base of the central stem.

The symbol was almost invisible unless you knew where to look: a circle split by jagged lines, bordered by an intricate lattice. It sent a strange chill through her.

She recognized it. Or at least, she thought she did.

Her mind raced back to the whispers she'd overheard in the library, the way the students had spoken about "them." The Syndicate. Could this be connected?

"Fascinating, isn't it?"

Isabella startled, nearly dropping her tray. She turned sharply to see Ben Foster leaning casually against the end of a long table, his usual air of detached cool firmly in place.

"What—what is?" she stammered, trying to mask her nerves.

Ben gestured lazily toward the chandelier. "The craftsmanship. It's impressive. You don't see ironwork like that much anymore."

Isabella hesitated, her eyes flicking back to the crest. "Yeah. I guess."

Ben's sharp gray eyes narrowed slightly as he studied her. "Something on your mind, Carter?"

She hesitated, debating whether to bring it up. Finally, she decided to test the waters. "Do you see that symbol? On the chandelier?"

Ben followed her gaze, tilting his head slightly. "Hmm. Never noticed it before. What about it?"

"It looks familiar," Isabella said cautiously. "Like I've seen it somewhere else."

Ben shrugged, his expression unreadable. "Could be just a design. Lots of fancy places like this have custom crests. Adds to the whole prestige thing."

Isabella frowned. "But why would a chandelier need a crest? It seems... specific."

Ben's lips quirked into a faint smirk, but there was no humor in it. "You're thinking too hard, Carter. Let me guess—you're connecting it to some grand conspiracy?"

She stiffened at the word "conspiracy," her pulse quickening. "I didn't say that."

"You didn't have to," Ben replied, his voice dropping slightly. "Your face said it for you."

Isabella crossed her arms, feeling defensive. "You don't think it's strange? That symbol—it's not just random decoration. Someone put it there for a reason."

Ben sighed, stepping closer and lowering his voice. "Listen. You're new here, so let me give you some advice: not everything needs a reason. And even if it does, sometimes it's better not to know what that reason is."

"Why?" she pressed, her tone sharper than she intended.

"Because knowing things comes with strings," Ben said evenly. "And Barrington isn't the kind of place where you want to get tangled up in those."

Isabella's frustration boiled over. "You're just like Rachel. Always hinting at things but never actually explaining anything. Do you know something about this or not?"

Ben's smirk faded, and for a moment, his expression hardened. "I know enough to keep my head down. You should, too."

She stared at him, her chest tight with anger and confusion. "Why are you being so cryptic? If you know something, why not just tell me?"

"Because it won't help you," Ben said, his tone almost weary. "If anything, it'll just make things worse."

"Worse how?"

He hesitated, his gaze flicking around the dining hall. The room had emptied significantly, leaving them mostly alone. Even so, he leaned in slightly, his voice dropping to a near whisper. "This place has eyes, Carter. And ears. You've noticed that by now, haven't you?"

Her stomach twisted. She had. The cameras in the chandeliers, the strange silences in conversations, the whispers in the library. It all added up.

Ben straightened, his expression unreadable once more. "Just… don't get too curious. Curiosity doesn't end well for people here."

Isabella clenched her jaw. "Maybe I'm okay with taking that risk."

Ben's smirk returned, but it was tinged with something darker. "Sure. You say that now. But you'll learn. They make sure of that."

Without another word, he turned and walked away, leaving her standing alone under the chandelier.

Isabella looked up again at the crest, the faint chill in her chest now a steady ache. Ben's words rang in her ears, cryptic and infuriating. They make sure of that.

Whatever the symbol meant, she was sure of one thing—it wasn't just decoration. And she wasn't going to stop until she found out the truth.

Isabella hadn't meant to linger. The winding halls of Barrington often invited exploration, but tonight she had simply taken a wrong turn on her way back to her dorm. The corridors were unnervingly quiet at this hour, her footsteps muted by the thick carpeting. As she passed the door to one of the smaller faculty lounges, muffled voices brought her to a halt.

She froze. The voices were distinct, low but urgent. She recognized one immediately: Professor Thorne, his commanding timbre unmistakable. The other was unfamiliar, softer but equally intense.

"No, she doesn't know yet," Thorne said, his voice clipped. "And that's exactly how it needs to stay. At least for now."

Isabella's heart leapt to her throat. She stepped back, pressing herself against the wall just out of sight. Her pulse quickened as she strained to hear.

"You're sure she's the right one?" the other voice asked.

"She fits the profile," Thorne replied sharply. "The academics, the background, even the psychological markers. Everything lines up. The Syndicate has already flagged her."

Syndicate. There it was again. The word sent a shiver down her spine, as though the very air around it was charged with meaning.

"And you're certain she's unaware?" the second voice pressed.

"Positive," Thorne said with a touch of impatience. "She's still acclimating to the school, and as long as we manage her exposure, she'll remain oblivious. It's imperative we control the timing."

Isabella felt her breath hitch. She clenched her fists, trying to keep herself from making any noise. They were talking about someone—someone important. Was it her?

"And what if she starts asking questions?"

There was a pause, and Isabella could almost picture Thorne's cold, calculating expression.

"She already has," Thorne admitted. "A few minor curiosities, but nothing we can't deflect. I've had Foster monitoring her interactions."

Ben. They had Ben watching her? The weight of the realization pressed down on her chest, and she had to fight the urge to gasp.

"You trust Foster to handle this?" the other professor asked, skepticism evident in his tone.

"I trust him to follow orders," Thorne said evenly. "Besides, his connection to the Syndicate is well-documented. If he steps out of line, we'll know."

There was a moment of silence, and then the second voice asked, "And when the time comes? What happens then?"

Thorne's reply was colder than the autumn night outside. "When the time comes, she'll have no choice but to comply. They never do."

A chill raced down Isabella's spine. She pressed her back harder against the wall, her mind racing. Comply? Comply with what? What were they planning for her—or whoever they were discussing?

"Let's hope you're right," the second voice murmured.

"I'm always right," Thorne said with quiet confidence. "That's why the Syndicate entrusted me with this. Just ensure your part is ready when I need it."

Their voices began to fade, punctuated by the creak of chairs and the shuffle of papers. Isabella realized with a jolt that the meeting was ending. She couldn't risk being caught here, not now, not after what she'd overheard.

Turning quickly but silently, she darted down the hall, her shoes barely making a sound against the carpet. Her heart pounded in her ears, drowning out everything else as she rounded corner after corner, desperate to put distance between herself and the faculty lounge.

When she finally reached her dorm, she closed the door behind her and leaned against it, her chest heaving. The dim, comforting familiarity of the room felt foreign now, tainted by what she'd just heard.

The Syndicate. Chosen scholars. Compliance.

She sank onto her bed, clutching the edges of the blanket as if it could anchor her. The word "Syndicate" now carried weight, a dark and undeniable presence she could no longer ignore. Every cryptic warning, every hushed whisper, every evasive answer suddenly clicked into place, forming the outline of something massive and terrifying.

And then there was Ben. His cryptic behavior, his guarded words—it wasn't just him being difficult. He was part of it. Thorne had said as much. But was he complicit, or was he just another cog in the machine?

Isabella's mind swirled with possibilities, each more alarming than the last. She felt like a spider had spun an invisible web around her, its threads tightening with every discovery. How far did this Syndicate's influence stretch? And why did it seem to revolve around her?

Her scholarship, her presence at Barrington—it was all beginning to feel less like an achievement and more like a trap.

She stared out the window at the glowing campus beyond, its spires and arches now shadowed with suspicion. There were too many unanswered questions, and the answers, she feared, would only lead to more danger.

But one thing was clear: she couldn't trust anyone. Not Rachel, not Ben, and certainly not Professor Thorne. If she wanted to understand what was happening, she would have to find the truth on her own.

And she had to do it before the Syndicate made her "comply."

Chapter 4
Silent Observers

Scene: Isabella struggles to adjust to the academic intensity of Barrington.

The morning sun poured into the lecture hall, glinting off the brass fixtures and casting a warm glow over the rows of polished wooden desks. Isabella sat in the middle row, her notebook open, pen poised, but her mind was lagging behind. The professor's voice was steady, delivering an endless stream of technical jargon and references to texts she hadn't read.

"...and as we see in Harrington's second treatise on systemic hierarchies, the convergence of the economic and sociological paradigms is inevitable. Miss Carter, do you agree?"

Isabella blinked, her stomach flipping. The professor—Dr. Marlowe, an intimidating figure with sharp glasses and a sharper tone—was staring directly at her. Several of her classmates turned to look as well, their expressions ranging from amused to mildly curious.

"I—uh—" Isabella's cheeks burned as she fumbled for a response. "I think it's... plausible?"

Dr. Marlowe arched an eyebrow, her expression unreadable. "Plausible. An interesting choice of words. Would you care to elaborate?"

Isabella's mind scrambled for an anchor, anything that might help her out of the spotlight. "Well, um... it makes sense in theory, but the practical applications might... vary depending on the context?"

A soft chuckle rippled through the room. Isabella gripped her pen tighter, feeling like the air around her had thickened.

"An admirable attempt," Dr. Marlowe said, her tone neutral but dismissive. She turned to another student. "Mr. Armitage, perhaps you can shed some light on the matter?"

A tall boy with perfectly tousled hair and a blazer that screamed old money leaned back in his chair, speaking with the practiced ease of someone used to being heard. "It's all about the balance of power, really. Harrington argues that economic structures inevitably dominate because they align with natural sociological hierarchies. The practicality, therefore, isn't a variable—it's a certainty."

"Excellent, Mr. Armitage," Dr. Marlowe said with a rare smile. "Precisely the point I was hoping to highlight."

Isabella sank lower in her seat, her pulse pounding in her ears. Around her, her peers nodded along, a chorus of silent agreement. She caught snippets of whispers.

"Classic Armitage. Always on point."

"Not a bad take, but he's quoted that line before."

"Carter looked totally lost."

The last comment stung, though it wasn't wrong. Isabella knew she was out of her depth. Everyone here seemed to come from a world she barely understood—a world of private tutors, family legacies, and exclusive networks. She could hear it in their conversations, too, during the rare lulls between classes.

"Are you interning with Morrow & Sons this summer?" one girl asked the boy seated next to her.

He nodded, casually flipping through his notes. "Yeah, Dad said it's good for building contacts before grad school."

"Lucky," the girl sighed. "I'm stuck at the family firm again. At least the perks are nice—penthouse in the city, full staff."

Isabella stared at her blank page, her pen idle. Internships? Penthouses? She couldn't even think past the mountain of reading assignments piling up, let alone plan a career built on connections she didn't have.

"You're Carter, right?" A voice interrupted her thoughts. It was the boy next to her—sharp jawline, an air of self-assurance, and an expensive watch that probably cost more than her entire wardrobe. "Scholarship student?"

The question wasn't cruel, but it wasn't kind either. It felt like a label, not a conversation starter.

"Yeah," Isabella said tightly, hoping he'd leave it at that.

He didn't. "Must be tough. Barrington's not exactly built for outsiders."

Isabella frowned. "I can manage."

The boy smirked, leaning back in his chair. "Sure you can. Just don't get caught falling behind. Professors here have high expectations, and they don't slow down for anyone."

Before she could reply, the professor's voice cut through the room again, and the conversation ended. But the boy's words lingered, intertwining with her own doubts. After class, Isabella trudged toward the library, hoping to catch up on the reading she'd fallen behind on. But as she passed through the arched corridor, her eyes caught something unusual—a small, almost imperceptible lens embedded in the corner where the wall met the ceiling. A camera.

Her stomach twisted. She'd noticed them before—outside the dining hall, near the quad—but now that she was looking, they seemed to be everywhere. She wondered how many eyes watched her stumble through her days at Barrington, unseen and unrelenting.

Her thoughts circled back to the whispers in the library, to Rachel's warning to "keep her head down." The cameras weren't just for security; they were part of something bigger. Something she was slowly beginning to understand but didn't yet have the words for. Taking a deep breath, Isabella pushed through the library doors and found a secluded corner. For now, she would bury herself in the reading and try to catch up. But the questions lingered, unanswered and gnawing at the edges of her mind. Barrington wasn't built for outsiders, the boy had said.

He was right, but Isabella wasn't planning to stay an outsider for long.

The library was quieter than usual, the muffled hum of voices from earlier replaced by the faint scratch of pen on paper and the occasional shuffle of pages. Isabella sat at a corner table, her notebook open but empty. The words on the page of her borrowed textbook blurred as her thoughts drifted. She couldn't shake the feeling of being watched, the lingering unease from the cameras she'd noticed in the corridors earlier.

"Mind if I join?" Rachel's cheerful voice broke the silence. Without waiting for a reply, she slid into the seat across from Isabella, setting down a precariously stacked pile of books.

"Sure," Isabella murmured, grateful for the distraction.

Rachel tilted her head, studying her. "You okay? You've got that 'I've seen a ghost' look again."

Isabella hesitated, her pen tapping absently against the edge of the notebook. "Do you ever feel like… someone's watching you?"

Rachel's brows furrowed briefly before a sly grin spread across her face. "What, like the professors? Or are we talking about something juicier?"

"Neither," Isabella said, her voice lowering instinctively. "I mean… around campus. Like, actually being watched."

Rachel's grin faltered. She leaned back, crossing her arms as her gaze flicked toward the chandelier above their table. "Ah, you've noticed them."

"Them?" Isabella asked, her voice tightening.

Rachel tapped the side of her temple, then nodded toward the chandelier. "The cameras."

Isabella's eyes widened. "There are cameras? In the chandeliers?"

Rachel smirked. "Not just the chandeliers. They're everywhere. Hallways, common areas, even the quad. Probably the dorms too."

"The dorms?" Isabella's voice rose slightly before she caught herself, glancing nervously around the library.

"Shh," Rachel said, holding up a finger to her lips. "It's not a secret exactly, but it's also not something people like to talk about. Kind of an open secret."

"That's insane," Isabella whispered. "Why would they need that much surveillance? It's a school, not a military base."

Rachel shrugged, her casual demeanor unconvincing. "Barrington has its quirks. Besides, they say it's for 'security.' You know, protecting all the precious rich kids."

Isabella frowned, leaning in closer. "You don't actually believe that, do you?"

Rachel hesitated, her fingers tracing the edge of one of her books. "Let's just say I don't ask too many questions. And I wouldn't recommend you do either."

"That's what everyone keeps saying," Isabella muttered, frustration creeping into her tone. "Why is everyone so afraid to talk about what's actually going on here?"

Rachel sighed, glancing around before lowering her voice further. "Look, you're new, so let me give you some advice. Barrington isn't like other schools. The surveillance, the rules, the way people act—it's all... different. And if you want to survive here, you've got to learn to play along."

"Play along?" Isabella repeated, incredulous. "How am I supposed to ignore something like this?"

Rachel's gaze softened, but her tone remained firm. "You think you're the first person to notice? Trust me, curiosity doesn't end well around here. The cameras aren't just there to catch people breaking rules. They're there to remind you that someone's always watching. And they want you to know it."

The weight of Rachel's words settled over Isabella like a heavy blanket. She shifted uncomfortably in her seat, her mind racing. "But who's 'they'? Who's behind all of this?"

Rachel gave a small, bitter laugh. "You think I know? All I know is that the second you start poking at it, you're on their radar. And trust me, that's not where you want to be."

Isabella looked up at the chandelier, her stomach twisting as she imagined unseen eyes tracking her every move. "This is insane."

"Welcome to Barrington," Rachel said dryly. "Where the tuition buys you more than just a fancy education. It buys you into a system. And not everyone gets out unscathed."

Isabella stared at Rachel, trying to gauge how serious she was. But Rachel's usual playful expression was gone, replaced by something colder, more cautious.

"Why are you telling me this?" Isabella asked quietly.

Rachel leaned forward, her voice dropping to a near-whisper. "Because you're one of the scholarship kids. That means they're watching you even more closely than the rest of us. You can't afford to slip up."

"I don't understand," Isabella said, her voice shaking slightly. "Why would they care about me? I'm nobody."

"That's what they want you to think," Rachel said, her tone grim. "But trust me, nobody here is just nobody."

The silence between them stretched, thick with unspoken tension. Isabella looked back down at her notebook, the blank page suddenly feeling like a metaphor for her own ignorance. She had come to Barrington thinking it was an opportunity, a chance to escape her old life and prove herself. But now, it felt like she had walked into a trap, one she didn't fully understand.

Rachel broke the silence, her voice lighter but still tinged with caution. "Anyway, just… keep your head down, okay? Focus on your classes, don't stand out too much. You'll be fine."

Isabella nodded slowly, though her mind was far from settled. The cameras, the whispers, the warnings—it all painted a picture of a school that was much more than it seemed. And she wasn't sure how much longer she could ignore it.

The dimly lit common room buzzed with low murmurs and occasional laughter. Most of the students were scattered across the plush chairs and couches, engrossed in quiet conversations or half-heartedly flipping through textbooks. Isabella sat at a table by the window, her back turned to the room, pretending to focus on her notes. In truth, her pen hovered uselessly over the page as she strained to listen to the group of students gathered a few seats away.

"Did you get the note?" a girl whispered, her voice so low that Isabella almost missed it. She recognized the speaker—Chloe, another scholarship student who rarely spoke in class but always seemed to be watching.

"Yeah," a boy replied, his tone sharp with worry. "Slipped under my door last night. 'Maintain discretion.' That's all it said."

Chloe huffed softly. "Mine said, 'Avoid unnecessary attention.' What does that even mean? Everything here feels like unnecessary attention."

Another boy spoke, his voice rough with tension. Isabella thought his name might have been Marcus. "It means they're watching us. Like, really watching. I mean, it's not just our grades they care about."

"Of course they're watching us," Chloe snapped. "That's been obvious since day one. But why? What are they looking for?"

"That's the part that freaks me out," Marcus said. "I don't think they're just looking. I think they're waiting for us to screw up. Or, worse, testing us."

Testing us. The words sent a chill through Isabella. She shifted slightly in her chair, careful not to make a sound. She could feel her heart racing, but she forced herself to keep still.

Another girl, one Isabella didn't recognize, leaned in closer to the group. "Do you think it's the Syndicate?" she whispered.

The table went quiet. Even Chloe, who seemed to have a sharp comment for everything, didn't reply immediately. Finally, Marcus broke the silence.

"Who else would it be?" he said, his voice barely audible. "The professors? Sure, maybe they're part of it, but this feels… bigger."

"Bigger how?" Chloe pressed, though her voice wavered slightly.

Marcus leaned forward, his elbows resting on the table. "Think about it. The cameras, the cryptic warnings, the way they pair us with mentors who seem more interested in our personal lives than our academics. It's all connected. They're shaping us for something."

"Shaping us for what?" Chloe asked, her frustration bubbling to the surface. "A life of paranoia?"

"I don't know," Marcus admitted. "But it's not just paranoia. There's a reason they brought us here, and it's not just because we're smart or talented. There's something else they're looking for."

The girl who had mentioned the Syndicate spoke up again, her voice shaky. "Do you think they already know? Like, about our... backgrounds?"

"Of course they do," Chloe said. "They knew before we even set foot on campus. That's why we're here. They handpicked us."

Marcus frowned, glancing around the room. His eyes lingered for a moment on Isabella's back, and she felt a prickle of panic. Did he know she was listening?

"They don't just pick you for academics," Marcus said after a moment. "They pick you for what they can use."

"What does that mean?" Chloe asked, though her tone suggested she didn't want an answer.

Marcus shook his head. "It means whatever it is they're looking for, they already think we have it. And now they're just waiting for us to prove it—or fail."

Isabella's grip on her pen tightened. She'd heard enough. Rising slowly, she tucked her notebook under her arm and headed for the stairs, careful to avoid making eye contact with the group as she passed. Her pulse hammered in her ears, drowning out the low murmur of their continued conversation.

As she reached the hallway leading to her dorm room, the weight of what she'd heard settled over her like a heavy fog. The cryptic warnings, the surveillance, the uneasy tension that seemed to hang over every interaction—it wasn't just paranoia. It was deliberate, calculated.

And the Syndicate. The name kept surfacing, whispered like a ghost haunting the edges of every conversation she wasn't supposed to hear. If what Marcus and the others were saying was true, then the Syndicate wasn't just watching. They were controlling. Shaping. Testing.

Isabella opened the door to her room and shut it softly behind her, leaning against it as she tried to steady her breathing. She thought back to Rachel's warning earlier that day—"Keep your head down, don't ask too many questions." But how could she not? How could she ignore the growing sense that everything around her was a carefully constructed façade, one designed to pull her into something she didn't understand?

Sinking onto her bed, she stared at the blank wall across from her, her mind racing. Marcus had said they were being tested, that the Syndicate was waiting for them to prove something. But what if she didn't want to prove anything? What if she just wanted to survive?

Her fingers brushed against the edge of her notebook, and she opened it almost reflexively. The pages were filled with notes from her classes, but they felt distant now, irrelevant compared to the questions gnawing at her. What was the Syndicate really after? And why did it feel like her every move was leading her closer to a truth she wasn't ready to face?

Isabella sat stiffly in the small office, her hands resting uneasily in her lap. The air was warm but heavy, and the faint scent of leather and old books filled the space. Professor Thorne sat across from her, a faint smile playing on his lips as he flipped through a slim folder—her folder, she realized with a jolt. Her name was printed neatly at the top.

"So," Thorne began, his voice smooth and deliberate, "how are you finding Barrington so far?"

Isabella hesitated, unsure how to answer. "It's... challenging, but I'm managing."

Thorne chuckled softly, his eyes flicking up from the folder to meet hers. "That's a diplomatic response. You don't strike me as the type to settle for 'managing.'"

"I just mean it's a lot to adjust to," Isabella said quickly, her fingers curling around the edge of her chair. "But I'm doing my best."

"Your best." Thorne repeated the words slowly, as though tasting them. He closed the folder and leaned back, steepling his fingers under his chin. "Your professors have had very positive things to say about you already. Marlowe, in particular, was impressed by your analytical approach in her lecture yesterday."

Isabella's cheeks flushed at the mention of Dr. Marlowe's class. "I didn't think I did that well," she admitted.

"Nonsense," Thorne said, his tone genial but firm. "You've shown remarkable promise in your short time here. It's rare for a scholarship student to acclimate so quickly to Barrington's... unique demands."

Isabella shifted uncomfortably. There was something in his tone that felt off, as though there was a second meaning hidden beneath the surface. "I'm just trying to keep up," she said cautiously.

"And succeeding," Thorne said with a nod. "But success here isn't measured solely by academics, Isabella. You understand that, don't you?"

Her stomach twisted. She wasn't sure how to respond, so she nodded hesitantly. "I think so."

Thorne smiled, though it didn't reach his eyes. "Barrington is a place that molds its students, shapes them into individuals capable of great things. But that process requires more than intelligence or hard work. It requires... alignment."

"Alignment?" Isabella echoed, her voice faint.

Thorne tilted his head slightly, studying her. "A willingness to adapt. To embrace the values and expectations of this institution. To trust that those in positions of authority have your best interests at heart."

"I do trust that," Isabella said quickly, though the words felt hollow as they left her mouth.

Thorne's smile widened, and he nodded approvingly. "Good. Trust is essential here. Barrington's standards are high, and we expect our students to rise to meet them. But we also expect loyalty. Not just to the school, but to the ideals it represents."

"I understand," Isabella said, though she wasn't sure she did.

Thorne leaned forward slightly, his eyes narrowing. "Do you? Because loyalty is not just about following rules, Isabella. It's about belief. Belief in the system, in the process, in the people who guide it."

Isabella's throat tightened. "I believe in working hard and doing what's expected of me."

"That's a good start," Thorne said, his voice soft but pointed. "But let me be clear: there are eyes on you, as there are on all our students. Barrington sees potential in you, Isabella. Great potential. But with that potential comes scrutiny."

"Scrutiny?" she asked, her voice barely above a whisper.

Thorne nodded slowly. "Think of it as... attention. We want to see how you navigate challenges, how you respond to adversity, how you conduct yourself. Everything you do here contributes to the person you will become."

Isabella forced herself to hold his gaze, though her heart was pounding. "I'll do my best."

"I have no doubt you will," Thorne said smoothly, leaning back again. "You're a bright young woman, Isabella. But brightness, like a flame, must be carefully tended. Too much exposure, and it can burn out. Too little, and it flickers away."

She swallowed hard, unsure how to respond. Thorne seemed to sense her unease and stood, signaling the end of their conversation.

"I'm glad we had this talk," he said, extending a hand toward her. "Consider it a... reminder that you're not alone in your journey here. There are people watching, guiding, ensuring you reach your full potential."

Isabella rose shakily, taking his hand in a brief, perfunctory shake. "Thank you, Professor Thorne."

His smile returned, sharp and inscrutable. "You're welcome, Miss Carter. I look forward to seeing what you accomplish."

As she left the office, her thoughts churned like a storm. Thorne's words echoed in her mind—scrutiny, alignment, loyalty. She couldn't shake the feeling that every step she took at Barrington was being monitored, judged. The warmth of his praise felt less like encouragement and more like a warning.

She pulled her jacket tighter around herself as she walked down the corridor, the shadows from the high windows stretching long and thin across the marble floor. Thorne's voice rang in her ears: "There are eyes on you." And for the first time since arriving at Barrington, Isabella wondered if she'd made a terrible mistake.

Chapter 5
Warnings in the Dark

The announcement was abrupt. The scholarship student's name was posted on the notice board in the main hall, a plain white paper among the usual clutter of club flyers and event schedules. **"Effective immediately, William Harker has been withdrawn from Barrington College."** The words were simple, clinical, devoid of explanation.

Isabella spotted the notice during her morning walk to the library. She stopped in her tracks, the weight of the words sinking into her chest. William Harker—she knew the name vaguely. He was another scholarship student, one of the quieter ones, always hovering at the edge of group discussions. Now, apparently, he was gone.

By lunchtime, the notice was the only topic of conversation in the cafeteria.

"Did you hear?" a girl whispered, leaning toward her friends. "Harker's gone. Just like that."

"What happened?" another asked, her voice low but tinged with excitement. "Did he fail his classes?"

"No way," a boy interjected. "Harker was one of the smart ones. Straight A's, if you believe the rumors."

"Then what?" the girl pressed.

The boy glanced around conspiratorially before lowering his voice. "I heard he broke a rule. Something serious."

"Like what?" the second girl asked, wide-eyed.

"No one knows," he said with a shrug. "But whatever it was, it must've been bad. They don't just kick people out like that."

At a nearby table, Isabella sat frozen, her fork hovering over her plate. The conversations blurred together, snippets of speculation weaving an ominous narrative.

"They say he didn't even pack his things," someone murmured. "Just disappeared overnight."

"Do you think the Syndicate had anything to do with it?" another voice whispered.

Isabella's grip on her fork tightened. The Syndicate again. The name kept creeping into conversations, a shadow lingering over every unexplained event at Barrington. She forced herself to take a bite of her food, though her appetite had vanished.

After lunch, Isabella found herself wandering aimlessly through the quad, her thoughts racing. The campus felt heavier today, its usual hum of activity undercut by a strange, uneasy silence. She spotted Rachel sitting on a bench, scrolling idly through her phone, and made her way over.

"You heard about Harker, right?" Isabella asked as she sat down beside her.

Rachel glanced up, her expression carefully neutral. "Hard not to. Everyone's talking about it."

"What do you think happened?" Isabella asked.

Rachel hesitated, her fingers tapping lightly against her phone. "He probably broke a rule," she said finally. "Barrington doesn't tolerate rule-breakers."

"Yeah, but what rule?" Isabella pressed. "And why did they have to withdraw him so suddenly? It doesn't make sense."

Rachel's eyes darted around the quad before she leaned in slightly. "Things don't have to make sense here, Isabella. Not to us, anyway. This place has its own rules—unwritten ones. And if you break them, you don't get a second chance."

Isabella frowned. "But that's not fair. How are we supposed to follow rules we don't even know about?"

Rachel shrugged, her expression unreadable. "Fairness doesn't matter. Compliance does."

Isabella leaned back, her mind churning. "Do you think the Syndicate had something to do with it?" she asked quietly.

Rachel's jaw tightened. "I think you should stop asking questions like that."

"But—"

"I'm serious," Rachel interrupted, her voice firm. "Whatever happened to Harker, it's none of our business. And if you want to stay here, you'll keep it that way."

The warning hung in the air between them, heavy and unspoken. Isabella looked away, her gaze drifting toward the library in the distance. The cameras she'd noticed earlier seemed more oppressive now, their presence a constant reminder that someone, somewhere, was always watching.

That night, the dorm was quieter than usual. Even the students who usually stayed up late chatting in the common room seemed subdued, their laughter muted and their conversations brief. Isabella lay in bed, staring at the ceiling, her thoughts spinning. What had William Harker done to warrant such swift and total removal? Was it a warning to the other scholarship students? Or was there something more sinister at play?

The Syndicate's name echoed in her mind again, a dark thread weaving through every strange occurrence at Barrington. Rachel's words came back to her: **"Fairness doesn't matter. Compliance does."** Isabella felt a chill run down her spine.

She turned over, pulling the blanket tighter around her. Sleep didn't come easily, her mind plagued by questions she couldn't answer and fears she couldn't shake. Whatever had happened to William Harker, one thing was certain—it wasn't just an isolated incident. It was a message. And Isabella couldn't help but wonder how long it would be before that message was meant for her.

The late afternoon sun streamed through the tall windows of the student lounge, casting warm patches of light across the worn leather couches and polished tables. Isabella sat with her notebook open in front of her, the pages covered in half-written sentences and disjointed questions. Her pen hovered above the paper, but her focus was elsewhere—her thoughts circling back to William Harker and the unanswered questions surrounding his abrupt departure.

"Still obsessing?" Rachel's voice pulled her back to reality. She stood nearby, a steaming mug of coffee in hand, her head tilted in that familiar way that suggested both curiosity and mild exasperation.

"Not obsessing," Isabella replied defensively, though the lie was obvious. "Just... thinking."

Rachel snorted softly and slid into the seat across from her. "You've got that look again. Like you're trying to solve the world's biggest mystery."

"It doesn't bother you?" Isabella asked, leaning forward slightly. "Harker's gone, and no one seems to know why. Or care."

Rachel took a slow sip of her coffee, her gaze steady on Isabella. "People care. They just know better than to talk about it."

"Why?" Isabella pressed. "What's the harm in asking questions?"

Rachel set her mug down with deliberate care, her expression sharpening. "Because questions have consequences here. Haven't you figured that out yet?"

The weight of her words hung in the air, and Isabella shifted uncomfortably. "It's not like I'm accusing anyone of anything. I just want to understand."

"That's exactly the problem," Rachel said, her tone dropping. "Understanding isn't part of the deal at Barrington. You're not here to figure out how things work. You're here to survive."

"Survive?" Isabella repeated, a faint chill creeping down her spine. "What does that even mean?"

Rachel leaned back in her chair, her eyes narrowing slightly. "It means you keep your head down, you do your work, and you don't draw attention to yourself. That's how you stay out of trouble."

Isabella frowned. "But that's not fair. If they're watching us, if they're punishing people like Harker, then shouldn't we at least know why?"

Rachel's expression softened slightly, but her tone remained firm. "Life's not fair, Carter. And Barrington definitely isn't. If you keep poking at things that don't concern you, you're going to end up just like Harker."

"Do you know what he did?" Isabella asked, her voice dropping to a whisper.

Rachel's jaw tightened, and for a moment, she didn't answer. When she finally spoke, her voice was quieter, almost resigned. "No. But it doesn't matter. Whatever it was, it was enough. And that's all you need to know."

Isabella looked down at her notebook, the questions she'd written earlier suddenly feeling dangerous, like evidence of a crime she hadn't realized she was committing. "You really think it's that bad?"

Rachel's gaze hardened. "I know it is. Look, I get it. You're new, and you think this place is just a school with a few weird rules. But it's not. Barrington's... different. The people in charge here, the ones who make the rules—they're not interested in fairness or explanations. They're interested in control."

The words sent a shiver through Isabella. She closed her notebook slowly, her mind racing. "But how can you just accept that? Don't you want to know the truth?"

Rachel shook her head, her lips pressing into a thin line. "I used to. And then I realized the truth doesn't matter. It's not going to change anything, and it's not going to help you. The only thing that matters is staying under the radar."

Isabella's chest tightened. She felt like a bird trapped in a cage she hadn't even noticed until now. "That's not a way to live."

"It's the only way to survive," Rachel said firmly. She reached for her coffee and stood, her voice softening as she added, "Just... be careful, okay? You're smarter than most people here, but that's not always a good thing."

Isabella watched her leave, the sound of her footsteps fading into the background hum of the lounge. The silence that followed felt heavier, pressing down on her like a weight she couldn't shake. She looked back at her notebook, the questions staring back at her like an accusation.

Was Rachel right? Was it better to stay quiet, to ignore the warning signs and hope for the best? Or was there a way to uncover the truth without putting herself in danger?

She wasn't sure. But one thing was certain: Barrington wasn't just a school. It was a game, and she was beginning to realize just how high the stakes really were.

The campus was unusually quiet as Isabella walked across the quad, the crisp evening air biting at her cheeks. The dim light from the lampposts cast long, wavering shadows across the brick pathways, making the familiar scenery feel foreign and uninviting. She spotted Ben leaning against the low stone wall near the fountain, hands in his pockets, his usual air of detachment amplified in the eerie stillness.

"You look like you've got something to say," Ben said as she approached, not bothering to look up.

Isabella stopped a few feet away, crossing her arms tightly over her chest. "Maybe I do. Are you going to listen, or are you just going to keep pretending nothing's wrong?"

Ben finally glanced up, his sharp gray eyes narrowing slightly. "Depends. Are we talking about Harker?"

"What else?" Isabella shot back, her frustration bubbling to the surface. "Everyone's acting like his disappearance is normal. Like it's just another day at Barrington."

"It is normal," Ben said evenly, his tone almost bored. "Normal for this place, anyway."

"That's not an answer," Isabella snapped.

"It's the only answer you're going to get," Ben replied. He straightened up and turned to face her fully, his expression unreadable. "What do you want me to say, Carter? That this school is screwed up? That we're all just pawns in some bigger game? You already know that."

"Maybe I want to hear it from someone else for a change," Isabella said, her voice softening slightly. "You've been here longer than me. You must know more than you're letting on."

Ben's jaw tightened, and he looked away, his hands still buried deep in his pockets. "Knowing more doesn't help. It just makes you a target."

"Is that what happened to Harker?" Isabella asked, stepping closer. "Did he know too much?"

Ben let out a short, humorless laugh. "Harker was stupid. He thought he could play their game and win. That's not how it works here."

"So you do know what happened," Isabella pressed.

"I know enough," Ben said, his voice low and edged with warning. "And you'd be smart to stop asking questions."

Isabella narrowed her eyes. "Why are you being so cryptic? If you know something, just tell me. You can't seriously expect me to keep my head down when everything around here feels... wrong."

Ben sighed, dragging a hand through his dark hair. "You really don't get it, do you? They don't care about what feels wrong. They care about control. And if you step out of line, even once, they'll remind you exactly who's in charge."

"Who's 'they'?" Isabella asked, her voice barely above a whisper.

Ben hesitated, his gaze flicking toward the darkened windows of the administration building. "The Syndicate. The professors. The administration. Take your pick. They're all part of the same machine."

"And you've been part of it too, haven't you?" Isabella said, the realization hitting her like a punch to the gut. "That's why you're so careful. You're not just keeping your head down—you're playing along."

Ben's expression darkened, but he didn't deny it. "I've been watched since my first year," he said quietly. "Every move I make, every word I say—it's all under a microscope. And it's not just me. It's everyone."

Isabella stared at him, her chest tightening. "Why? What are they looking for?"

"They're looking for cracks," Ben said, his voice hardening. "Weaknesses. Reasons to pull you in deeper or push you out completely. And if you give them a reason, even for a second, you're done."

"Is that what happened to you?" Isabella asked cautiously. "Did you give them a reason?"

Ben's lips curved into a bitter smile. "I gave them just enough to keep them satisfied. That's the trick, Carter. You have to give them just enough to make them think you're playing along, but not so much that they can use it against you."

Isabella felt a shiver run down her spine. "That sounds exhausting."

"It is," Ben admitted. "But it's better than the alternative."

"And what's the alternative?" Isabella asked, though she wasn't sure she wanted to hear the answer.

Ben's eyes met hers, and for the first time, she saw a flicker of vulnerability behind his usual guarded expression. "Ask Harker," he said simply. "Oh wait, you can't."

The words hit her like a slap, and she took a step back, her mind racing. Ben turned away, his posture tense as he stared out at the fountain.

"Look," he said after a moment, his voice softer now. "I get it. You want answers. But trust me, Carter, you don't want the ones you're looking for. Not here. Not now."

"Then what am I supposed to do?" Isabella asked, her voice trembling with frustration.

Ben turned back to her, his expression unreadable once more. "You do what everyone else does. You survive."

And with that, he walked away, leaving Isabella alone in the growing darkness. She stood there for a long time, her thoughts spinning. She didn't want to just survive. She wanted to understand. But as Ben's warning echoed in her mind, she realized that understanding might come at a cost she wasn't ready to pay.

Isabella pushed open the door to her dorm room, her shoulders heavy with the weight of the day. The quiet hum of campus life had given way to an eerie stillness, and as the door clicked shut behind her, the faintest sense of unease crept up her spine. She flicked on the desk lamp, the soft glow illuminating the small, neatly arranged space she'd come to call her own.

Setting her bag down, she reached for her notebook, flipping through the pages of cryptic notes and half-formed theories. Her mind drifted back to her earlier conversation with Ben, his words a warning and a challenge all at once: **"They're watching. Always."**

She glanced around the room, her gaze lingering on the corners and shadows. The thought had struck her earlier, an unsettling notion she'd tried to push aside. But now it was unavoidable. If the campus hallways and common areas were littered with surveillance cameras, why would the dorms be any different?

With a steadying breath, she stood and began inspecting the room. She started with the obvious places—the corners of the ceiling, the base of the bookshelf—but found nothing. Her heart rate quickened as her search grew more meticulous.

She moved to the desk, running her fingers along its underside. Nothing. Her hands trembled slightly as she crouched down to check behind the radiator. Still nothing.

"This is ridiculous," she muttered to herself, rising to her feet. But as her eyes swept across the room again, they landed on the smoke detector mounted on the ceiling above her bed. It was small, unassuming, the kind of object easily overlooked.

A surge of dread washed over her as she grabbed her desk chair and dragged it beneath the device. Climbing up, she examined the smoke detector closely. Her fingers brushed against its surface, and she noticed a small, almost invisible seam along the edge.

Her breath hitched. Carefully, she twisted the device, and it came loose from its bracket with a soft click. Holding it in her hands, she turned it over—and froze.

A tiny lens stared back at her, embedded in the center of the smoke detector's underside.

"No," she whispered, her voice barely audible. Her pulse pounded in her ears as she stared at the camera, her mind racing. How long had it been there? Who was watching? What had they seen?

The sound of footsteps in the hallway made her jump, and she nearly dropped the device. She hurriedly replaced it in its bracket, twisting it back into place before stepping down from the chair. Her chest heaved as she leaned against the desk, trying to collect her thoughts.

A knock at the door made her flinch. "Isabella?"

She recognized Rachel's voice and exhaled shakily. Crossing the room, she opened the door a crack.

Rachel frowned at her, tilting her head. "You okay? You look like you've seen a ghost."

Isabella hesitated before stepping aside to let her in. "It's... nothing. Just a long day."

Rachel entered, her sharp gaze scanning the room. "You sure? You look like you're about to crawl out of your skin."

Isabella closed the door and turned to face her, the words tumbling out before she could stop herself. "There's a camera. In the smoke detector."

Rachel blinked, her expression hardening. "You checked?"

"Yes," Isabella said, her voice barely above a whisper. "I didn't want to believe it, but it's there. They're watching us. Even here."

Rachel sighed, running a hand through her hair. "Of course they are. You think this place has any boundaries?"

"How can you say that so calmly?" Isabella demanded, her frustration boiling over. "This isn't normal, Rachel. It's—"

"Of course it's not normal!" Rachel snapped, cutting her off. "But this is Barrington. This is how it works. You think you're the first person to figure it out? They've been doing this for years. Decades, probably."

Isabella stared at her, stunned. "And no one does anything about it?"

"What are we supposed to do?" Rachel asked, her voice softening. "Report it? To who? The same people who put the cameras there in the first place?"

The silence that followed was deafening. Isabella looked away, her hands balling into fists at her sides.

"I'm not just going to ignore this," she said finally, her voice steady despite the fear coursing through her.

Rachel sighed again, shaking her head. "You're braver than me, Carter. Or maybe just more reckless. Either way, be careful. If you push too hard, you'll end up like Harker. Or worse."

The mention of Harker sent a chill down Isabella's spine, but she refused to let it deter her. She met Rachel's gaze, her eyes burning with determination. "I'll be careful," she said. "But I'm not going to stop."

Rachel studied her for a long moment before nodding slowly. "Just don't say I didn't warn you."

As Rachel left, Isabella sat down on her bed, her mind racing. The camera above her was a constant, oppressive presence, but instead of fear, she felt a flicker of something stronger—resolve.

They were watching her. But she was watching them, too.

Chapter 6
The Price of Insight

The lecture hall was unusually quiet for Dr. Marlowe's philosophy seminar. Isabella sat near the middle of the room, her notebook open and pen poised. The professor's voice resonated through the space, weaving complex theories of ethical relativism and systemic hierarchies into a tapestry that felt impenetrable. Most students scribbled notes frantically, struggling to keep up, but Isabella found herself lost in thought, her mind darting between fragments of the lecture.

"Now," Dr. Marlowe said, pausing to survey the room, "can anyone explain how Harrington's convergence theory applies to the debate between utilitarianism and deontology?"

A heavy silence fell. Isabella glanced around, her classmates either avoiding eye contact or staring blankly at their notes. The tension in the room was palpable.

Dr. Marlowe's sharp gaze landed on Isabella. "Miss Carter?"

Isabella's heart skipped a beat. She hadn't been fully listening, at least not in the traditional sense. But the question seemed to unlock something in her mind, a puzzle snapping into place with startling clarity.

"Well," she began tentatively, her voice steady despite the nervous flutter in her chest, "Harrington's convergence theory argues that in any sufficiently complex system, competing ethical frameworks—like utilitarianism and deontology—tend to reconcile over time. The friction between them creates a synthesis, a new framework that incorporates elements of both."

Dr. Marlowe tilted her head, intrigued. "Go on."

Isabella swallowed, her confidence growing as she spoke. "For example, in large organizations, you see policies that prioritize outcomes, like maximizing efficiency or profit—classic utilitarian goals. But those same organizations often adopt strict codes of conduct to maintain order and fairness, which are more in line with deontological principles. Over time, these systems evolve to balance the two, creating a kind of ethical equilibrium."

The room was silent again, but this time it felt different. Eyes turned toward Isabella, not with amusement or skepticism, but with something closer to respect—or maybe envy.

"That's... an interesting interpretation," Dr. Marlowe said, her tone measured. "And what do you think drives this synthesis? Is it purely practical, or is there an inherent moral logic at play?"

Isabella hesitated, considering the question. "I think it starts as a practical necessity. Systems adapt to survive. But as those adaptations solidify, they take on a moral dimension. People begin to believe in the rules they've created, even if those rules were originally just pragmatic solutions."

Dr. Marlowe's lips curved into a faint smile, though her eyes held a sharper edge. "You're suggesting that morality is, at its core, a byproduct of survival. An interesting—and provocative—theory."

Isabella nodded slowly. "I think so. But it also explains why morality can feel so rigid sometimes. Once a system stabilizes, people resist change, even when the original purpose of the rules no longer applies."

"Fascinating," Dr. Marlowe said, her gaze lingering on Isabella a moment longer than necessary. "Class, I'd encourage you all to consider Miss Carter's analysis as you work on your essays this week. It's not often we see this level of synthesis in first-year students."

A murmur rippled through the room. Isabella felt a flush of warmth creep up her neck, part pride and part unease. She ducked her head, pretending to jot down a note as the professor resumed her lecture.

After class, as students filed out of the room, Isabella lingered at her desk, gathering her things slowly. Dr. Marlowe approached, her sharp heels clicking softly against the floor.

"Miss Carter," she said, her tone quieter now, almost conspiratorial.

Isabella looked up, startled. "Yes, Professor?"

"You have a gift," Marlowe said, her gaze piercing. "The way you connected those theories today—it's not something I see often. Certainly not from someone with your background."

"My background?" Isabella repeated, frowning.

Marlowe's smile was tight, calculated. "Scholarship students tend to excel in practical areas, but theoretical analysis requires a certain... intuition. Yours is exceptional."

"Thank you," Isabella said, unsure whether the compliment was genuine or something else entirely.

"Have you given much thought to what you want to achieve here at Barrington?" Marlowe asked, her tone casual but probing.

"I'm still figuring that out," Isabella admitted.

"Hmm." Marlowe studied her for a moment longer before nodding. "Well, keep in mind that opportunities here often depend on more than just academic success. The right connections, the right attitudes—those are just as important."

Isabella stiffened slightly. "I'll keep that in mind."

Marlowe's smile returned, sharper this time. "Good. I look forward to seeing what you accomplish." With that, she turned and walked away, her heels echoing down the hallway.

Isabella sat frozen for a moment, her mind replaying the conversation. The professor's praise had felt genuine, but there was something beneath it, a layer of expectation—or maybe warning—that unsettled her. The room, once a place of intellectual exploration, now felt like a stage, every word and action scrutinized under a hidden spotlight.

As she left the lecture hall, her thoughts swirled with questions she couldn't yet answer. What had Marlowe meant by "the right connections"? And why did her compliment feel less like an acknowledgment of talent and more like an invitation—or a test?

The campus stretched out before her, serene and deceptive in its beauty. Isabella knew now that she was being noticed. And she wasn't sure whether that was a blessing or a curse.

The library was quiet except for the faint rustle of pages turning and the occasional scrape of a chair against the floor. Isabella sat hunched over a thick textbook, its margins crammed with tiny, indecipherable annotations. Her notebook was open beside her, but the page remained blank. The dense language of the text seemed to blur and dance in front of her eyes, defying comprehension.

She sighed, leaning back in frustration. Her head ached from hours of reading, but she knew she couldn't afford to stop. The assignment was due in two days, and she was barely halfway through the material.

"Hey," Rachel's voice broke through her thoughts, light and teasing. "You look like you're trying to crack the Da Vinci Code over here."

Isabella glanced up, managing a weak smile. "Feels like it."

Rachel slid into the seat across from her, a latte in hand. "You've been at this for hours. Take a break before your brain melts."

"I can't," Isabella muttered, gesturing to the book. "If I don't finish this, Marlowe's going to eat me alive."

Rachel smirked. "Marlowe eats everyone alive. It's kind of her thing. But seriously, you're going to burn yourself out."

"I'm fine," Isabella said, though her voice lacked conviction. She turned back to the textbook, willing herself to focus.

At first, the words remained stubbornly incomprehensible. But then something shifted. It was subtle at first—a flicker of clarity, like a light being switched on in the back of her mind. The sentences began to arrange themselves into patterns, the ideas linking together with startling precision. Concepts that had felt opaque moments ago now seemed obvious, their meaning unfolding with almost mathematical clarity.

She began to write, her pen flying across the page as she transcribed her thoughts. Her hand moved faster than her conscious mind, as though the ideas were pouring out of her without effort. The textbook no longer felt like an obstacle but a map, its intricate pathways revealing themselves in perfect detail.

Rachel watched her, her teasing smile fading. "Uh... Isabella?"

Isabella didn't respond. She was too engrossed, her focus so sharp it bordered on obsession. Her eyes darted across the text, her lips moving slightly as she muttered under her breath, piecing together connections she hadn't even realized she was capable of making.

"Isabella," Rachel said more firmly, leaning forward and snapping her fingers. "Hello? Earth to Carter."

Isabella blinked, her pen pausing mid-word. She looked up, her expression dazed. "What?"

"What was that?" Rachel asked, her brow furrowing. "You were in some kind of... trance."

"I was just..." Isabella trailed off, glancing down at her notebook. The page was filled with dense, detailed notes—far more than she'd expected to accomplish. She frowned, trying to piece together how she'd written so much in such a short amount of time.

Rachel's gaze flicked between the textbook and the notebook. "Did you seriously just figure all that out? In, like, five minutes?"

"I guess?" Isabella said uncertainly. "It just... clicked."

Rachel leaned back, crossing her arms. "Clicked? That's not normal, Carter. You were practically vibrating."

Isabella shifted uncomfortably. "I don't know what to tell you. It just... happens sometimes."

Rachel's eyes narrowed. "Define 'sometimes.'"

"It's hard to explain," Isabella admitted. "It's like… I'll be stuck on something, and then all of a sudden, it makes sense. Like someone flipped a switch in my brain."

Rachel stared at her for a moment, then shook her head. "That's not normal. And if I've learned anything about Barrington, it's that anything not normal gets noticed."

"I'm not trying to stand out," Isabella said defensively.

"Well, you're doing a pretty bad job of it," Rachel shot back. "Do you think Marlowe isn't going to notice if you turn in an essay that's miles ahead of everyone else's?"

"I can't just stop thinking," Isabella said, frustration creeping into her voice. "What do you want me to do? Dumb myself down?"

"I'm saying you need to be careful," Rachel said, her tone softening. "You're smart, Carter. Scary smart. But being smart here isn't always a good thing. People notice. And when people notice, so do… other people."

"What's that supposed to mean?" Isabella asked, narrowing her eyes.

Rachel sighed, glancing around the library as if checking for eavesdroppers. "It means this place has a way of turning strengths into weaknesses. If you stand out too much, someone's going to take an interest in you. And trust me, you don't want that kind of attention."

Isabella hesitated, her fingers tightening around her pen. "You really think it's that dangerous?"

"I know it is," Rachel said firmly. "You're good, Carter. Better than good. But you need to keep it under control. Blend in, play the game. Otherwise, you're going to end up like Harker."

The mention of Harker sent a chill down Isabella's spine. She looked down at her notes, the clarity she'd felt moments ago now tinged with unease.

"I'll... think about it," she said finally, her voice low.

"Do more than think about it," Rachel said, standing and grabbing her latte. "Survival here isn't just about being smart. It's about being smart enough to stay invisible."

As Rachel walked away, Isabella sat frozen, her mind racing. She stared at the notebook in front of her, the neatly written notes now feeling like evidence of something she couldn't quite name. The clarity that had felt so empowering moments ago now felt like a beacon, drawing eyes she couldn't see.

Blending in had never felt so impossible.

Isabella sat cross-legged on the floor of her dorm room, a dense puzzle book open in front of her. The room was dim, lit only by the glow of her desk lamp. She had dragged her chair to block the smoke detector camera overhead. Even if they were watching, she wasn't about to let them see this.

The puzzle stared back at her like a challenge, the kind she'd normally avoid. Rows of interconnected symbols and abstract clues stretched across the page, forming a web of logic she knew should take hours to untangle. But she wasn't in the mood for caution tonight.

"Okay," she muttered to herself, gripping her pencil tightly. "Let's see what this is all about."

She started slowly, letting her eyes trace the patterns. At first, it felt like a familiar kind of frustration—too many possibilities, too much to keep track of. Her pencil hovered uselessly over the page as her thoughts tangled.

Then, something shifted.

It began with a flicker of recognition, like catching a glimpse of a face in a crowd. The symbols on the page seemed to fall into place, forming a coherent pattern she hadn't noticed before. Her breathing slowed, her focus narrowing to a razor-sharp point as the puzzle began to unfold in her mind.

Her hand moved almost on its own, the pencil sketching out connections and solving equations with a speed that surprised even her. She flipped to the next page and the next, her movements growing faster, more confident. Each answer led seamlessly to the next clue, the logic behind the puzzle clicking into place as if it had always been obvious.

By the time she reached the final section, her hand was trembling. The room felt too warm, her pulse pounding in her ears. She ignored it, pushing forward as her pencil scrawled the last few calculations.

"Done," she whispered, dropping the pencil onto the book. She leaned back against the bed, staring at the finished puzzle. The page was filled with neat lines and symbols, every box accounted for.

She'd solved the entire thing in under fifteen minutes.

Her chest swelled with pride, but the triumph was short-lived. A sharp pain shot through her head, sudden and intense. She pressed her hands to her temples, wincing as the ache radiated behind her eyes.

"Ugh," she groaned, squeezing her eyes shut. The pain didn't fade; it only seemed to intensify, like a vice tightening around her skull.

There was a knock at the door.

"Isabella?" Rachel's voice called out from the hallway.

Isabella groaned again, louder this time, as she stumbled to her feet. She stumbled to the door and cracked it open, wincing at the bright hallway light.

Rachel frowned, stepping back slightly. "Whoa, are you okay? You look like you've been hit by a truck."

"I'm fine," Isabella muttered, her voice strained. "Just a headache."

Rachel pushed past her and stepped into the room, her eyes narrowing as she noticed the blocked smoke detector and the open puzzle book on the floor.

"Is this what you've been doing?" Rachel asked, crossing her arms. "No wonder you look like death warmed over."

"It's nothing," Isabella said, closing the door and leaning heavily against it. "Just a stupid puzzle."

Rachel snorted. "You expect me to believe that? You look like you ran a mental marathon."

Isabella hesitated, her hands still pressed to her temples. "I wanted to see if I could do it."

"And?" Rachel prompted, raising an eyebrow.

"And I did," Isabella admitted. "But it wasn't like before. It was... different."

"Different how?" Rachel asked, stepping closer.

"It's hard to explain," Isabella said, lowering her hands and meeting Rachel's gaze. "It was like... my brain just knew what to do. Everything made sense, even the stuff that shouldn't have. I didn't even have to think about it."

Rachel studied her for a moment, her expression unreadable. "And now you're paying for it."

"It's just a headache," Isabella said defensively.

"It's not just a headache, Carter," Rachel said sharply. "This isn't normal. Whatever's going on with you, it's taking a toll. And if you keep pushing yourself like this, you're going to break."

Isabella bristled. "I'm not going to break. I'm fine."

Rachel sighed, running a hand through her hair. "Look, I get it. You want to prove something—to yourself, to the professors, maybe even to the Syndicate. But you need to know your limits. Otherwise, they'll find them for you."

Isabella frowned, her headache easing slightly as Rachel's words sank in. "You really think they're watching me that closely?"

Rachel nodded. "I don't think, Carter. I know. And if they see you burning out, they're not going to help. They're going to use it against you."

The silence that followed was heavy, charged with unspoken tension. Isabella looked down at the puzzle book, her earlier triumph now tinged with unease.

"Just... be careful," Rachel said finally, her tone softening. "Whatever this is, it's not worth losing yourself over."

Isabella nodded slowly, though the knot in her chest refused to loosen. She wasn't sure what scared her more—the intensity of her newfound abilities or the price she might have to pay for them.

The faint echo of footsteps filled the corridor as Isabella walked toward Professor Thorne's office. The summons had come out of nowhere, an email marked **URGENT** that sent a prickle of unease through her. The door to his office stood ajar, revealing dark wood shelves lined with books and a faint glow from a desk lamp inside.

She knocked lightly. "Professor Thorne? You wanted to see me?"

"Come in, Miss Carter," his deep voice called. It was smooth, even pleasant, but it carried an undercurrent of authority that made Isabella's stomach tighten.

She stepped inside, clutching her notebook against her chest. Thorne stood by the window, looking out over the campus as the evening light painted the room in hues of gold and shadow. He turned, offering her a small, enigmatic smile.

"Thank you for coming so promptly," he said, gesturing toward the chair in front of his desk. "Please, have a seat."

Isabella obeyed, setting her notebook on her lap. "Is something wrong?" she asked cautiously.

"Not at all," Thorne replied, settling into his chair across from her. "In fact, quite the opposite. Your performance in class has been... noteworthy."

She blinked, unsure how to respond. "Thank you, Professor."

"It's rare," Thorne continued, folding his hands on the desk, "to see a first-year student demonstrate the level of analytical insight you've shown. Dr. Marlowe speaks highly of your contributions."

Isabella shifted uncomfortably. "I've just been trying to keep up."

Thorne smiled faintly, his eyes sharp and calculating. "Modesty is admirable, Miss Carter, but let's not downplay the facts. Your recent analysis of Harrington's convergence theory was not just insightful—it was exceptional."

Her pulse quickened. There was something unsettling about the way he spoke, as though he were probing for something beneath the surface.

"I appreciate the feedback," Isabella said, keeping her tone neutral. "But I'm sure other students are doing just as well."

"Perhaps," Thorne said, leaning back slightly. "But your particular aptitude is... unique. Wouldn't you agree?"

She hesitated, her grip tightening on her notebook. "I'm not sure what you mean."

Thorne's smile widened, though it didn't reach his eyes. "You have a way of seeing patterns that others miss. A clarity of thought that sets you apart. It's not just intelligence—it's intuition, the ability to synthesize complex ideas effortlessly."

Isabella's heart raced. He couldn't know about her puzzle-solving session the night before—or could he? "I just work hard," she said carefully.

Thorne chuckled softly. "Hard work is part of it, certainly. But there's more to it than that. Tell me, Isabella, have you ever felt as though certain problems simply… solved themselves in your mind?"

Her breath caught, and she forced herself to stay calm. "I don't know what you're talking about."

"Don't you?" Thorne's tone was gentle, almost conspiratorial. "Your scholarship, for example. Did you ever wonder why you were chosen?"

"I assumed it was based on my grades," she said, though the words felt hollow as they left her mouth.

"That's the official explanation," Thorne said with a faint smile. "But Barrington's scholarship program is more selective than most realize. We don't just look for academic excellence. We look for potential. For students who can offer... something more."

Isabella's throat tightened. "What kind of potential?"

Thorne's gaze held hers, unflinching. "The kind that can't be taught. The kind that makes you an asset in ways others aren't."

The word **asset** sent a chill down her spine. She shifted in her seat, her mind racing with unspoken questions. "I still don't understand," she said finally.

"You will," Thorne said, his tone suddenly brisk. "In time. For now, focus on your studies. Continue to excel, as you have been. And remember, Miss Carter, that we are watching with great interest."

The phrase hung in the air like a threat disguised as a compliment. Isabella nodded slowly, her palms damp against her notebook. "I'll... do my best."

"I have no doubt you will," Thorne said, standing to signal the end of the meeting. "That will be all for now."

She stood, clutching her notebook tightly as she turned to leave. But as she reached the door, Thorne's voice stopped her.

"Oh, and one more thing, Miss Carter."

She turned back, her pulse quickening. "Yes?"

Thorne's smile returned, sharper this time. "Be mindful of how much you reveal to others. Not everyone will appreciate your talents as much as we do."

The words were polite, almost pleasant, but the undertone was unmistakable. Isabella nodded once before slipping out of the office, her thoughts spinning.

The hallway felt colder than before, the shadows longer and darker. Thorne's cryptic remarks replayed in her mind, each word laced with layers she couldn't fully untangle. Her scholarship, her abilities, the way he spoke about potential—it was all connected to something bigger. Something she was only beginning to glimpse.

As she walked back to her dorm, one thought burned brighter than the rest: she wasn't just being watched. She was being evaluated.

Chapter 7
The Burden of Secrets

The air in the campus courtyard was thick with the scent of damp leaves and distant rain. Isabella sat on the edge of a stone bench, watching Ben pace a few steps away, his hands shoved deep into his jacket pockets. The courtyard was empty, save for the occasional gust of wind rustling the trees.

"You've been here longer than me," Isabella began, her voice steady despite the unease bubbling beneath the surface. "You must have noticed things."

Ben stopped pacing and glanced at her, his expression unreadable. "Noticed what?"

"You know what I'm talking about," Isabella said, her voice softening. "The cameras. The whispers. The way people disappear without a trace."

Ben let out a short, humorless laugh. "Took you long enough."

Isabella frowned. "So, you have noticed."

"Of course I've noticed," Ben replied, leaning against a nearby lamppost. "It's impossible not to. But noticing doesn't mean you can do anything about it."

She studied him for a moment, her curiosity growing. "How did you figure it out?"

Ben hesitated, his gaze drifting toward the empty pathway ahead. "My first year here," he began slowly, "I thought Barrington was everything it claimed to be. Elite. Exclusive. A place where the smartest and hardest-working students came to prove themselves."

"And?" Isabella prompted, leaning forward slightly.

"And I learned pretty quickly that's only part of the story," Ben said, his voice taking on a bitter edge. "There's another side to this place—one they don't put in the brochures."

He paused, running a hand through his dark hair. For a moment, Isabella thought he might not continue, but then he sighed and sat down on the bench beside her.

"There was this guy in my year," Ben said, his tone quieter now. "Ethan. Smart. Ambitious. One of those people who could charm their way through anything. He figured out pretty early that Barrington wasn't just about academics."

"What do you mean?" Isabella asked.

Ben's jaw tightened. "He started asking questions. About the scholarships, the surveillance, the strange rules no one ever explained. At first, it seemed harmless. But then he started poking too hard."

"Poking at what?" Isabella asked, her heart quickening.

"Whatever it is that makes this place tick," Ben said vaguely. "The Syndicate, the professors, the administration—they're all part of it. And Ethan thought he could figure it out."

"What happened to him?" Isabella asked, though she wasn't sure she wanted to know the answer.

Ben's expression darkened. "One day, he was here. The next, he wasn't. No explanation, no goodbyes. Just a quiet little note on the board: 'Withdrawn.' Same as Harker."

A chill ran down Isabella's spine. "Did you ever find out why?"

Ben shook his head. "No one talks about it. Not directly. But it's not hard to guess. He got too close to something he wasn't supposed to see."

"Why are you telling me this?" Isabella asked, her voice barely above a whisper.

Ben met her gaze, his eyes sharp and guarded. "Because you remind me of him."

Her breath caught. "I'm not trying to—"

"You don't have to try," Ben interrupted. "This place has a way of pulling you in, whether you want it to or not. And once you're in, it's hard to get out."

Isabella frowned, her thoughts racing. "Why didn't you warn him? Ethan, I mean."

"I did," Ben said, his voice tinged with regret. "But he didn't listen. He thought he was smarter than them. That he could beat them at their own game."

"Could he have?" Isabella asked, though she already suspected the answer.

Ben shook his head. "No one beats them. Not here. The best you can do is survive."

The words hung in the air between them, heavy and unspoken. Isabella looked away, her gaze falling on the darkened windows of the library in the distance. The weight of Ben's story settled over her, a grim reminder of the stakes she was only beginning to understand.

"So, what do you do?" Isabella asked finally. "How do you survive?"

Ben stood, shoving his hands back into his pockets. "You keep your head down. You play the game. And you don't ask questions you don't want answers to."

She watched him walk away, his figure disappearing into the shadows. For a moment, she felt more alone than ever. But as the silence of the courtyard pressed in around her, one thought burned in her mind: she couldn't just survive. She had to understand.

No matter the cost.

The cafeteria was quieter than usual, the hum of conversation dulled by the weight of recent events. Isabella sat across from Ben at a small corner table, her untouched tray of food between them. Ben leaned back in his chair, casually sipping a cup of coffee, his expression as unreadable as ever.

"You're awfully calm for someone who claims to know how dangerous this place is," Isabella said, breaking the silence.

Ben arched an eyebrow but didn't respond immediately. Instead, he set his cup down with deliberate care. "I don't recall claiming anything."

"You don't have to," Isabella shot back. "It's written all over you. You know more than you're letting on."

Ben smirked, leaning forward slightly. "And what makes you think that?"

"Because every time I ask you a real question, you dodge it," Isabella said, her tone sharp. "Like now."

Ben's smirk faltered, replaced by a flicker of something darker. He glanced around the cafeteria, his eyes scanning for anyone who might be listening. Satisfied they were alone, he leaned back again, crossing his arms.

"Fine," he said, his tone soft but edged with warning. "You want to know why I don't give you straight answers? Because straight answers are dangerous."

"For you, or for me?" Isabella asked, narrowing her eyes.

"For both of us," Ben replied evenly. "The less you know, the safer you are. Trust me."

Isabella frowned, frustration bubbling beneath the surface. "You keep saying that, but it doesn't make sense. If something's really going on here, don't I have the right to know?"

Ben's gaze hardened. "A right? Maybe. But a right doesn't mean it's smart. This isn't some mystery you can solve by asking the right questions. It's bigger than that."

"Then explain it to me," Isabella said, leaning forward. "What's so big that everyone's too afraid to talk about it?"

Ben sighed, dragging a hand through his hair. "Do you remember what I told you about Ethan?"

"Yes," Isabella said, her voice steady. "You said he asked too many questions. That he got too close to something he wasn't supposed to see."

Ben nodded. "And what happened to him?"

Isabella's stomach twisted. "He disappeared."

"Exactly," Ben said, his tone sharp. "And you think knowing more is going to make you safer? It won't. It'll make you a target."

"But what's the point of staying here if I don't understand what I'm up against?" Isabella asked, her voice rising slightly. "How am I supposed to survive if I don't know the rules?"

"The rules are simple," Ben said, his voice lowering. "Keep your head down. Don't stand out. Don't ask questions you don't want answers to."

"That's not good enough," Isabella said, her frustration boiling over. "I can't just bury my head in the sand and pretend everything's fine."

Ben's expression darkened, and for a moment, she thought he might walk away. But instead, he leaned forward, his voice dropping to a near whisper. "Do you think I don't want to tell you? That I don't want to help? I've seen what happens to people who dig too deep, Isabella. It's not just about disappearing. It's about losing yourself. Your future. Your mind. Everything."

The weight of his words hit her like a punch to the gut. She sat back, her heart pounding. "What happened to you?" she asked quietly.

Ben hesitated, his jaw tightening. "Let's just say I learned my lesson. And I've managed to stay out of trouble since. Barely."

Isabella stared at him, her frustration giving way to a mix of fear and sympathy. "But you're still here. You didn't leave."

"Not yet," Ben admitted, his voice softer now. "But I've thought about it. More than once."

"Then why stay?" Isabella asked.

Ben's smirk returned, though it was tinged with bitterness. "Because leaving isn't as easy as it sounds. And sometimes, surviving is all you can do."

The silence between them stretched, heavy with unspoken truths. Isabella looked down at her tray, her appetite long gone. She wanted to press him further, to demand real answers, but the look in his eyes stopped her.

"Just... be careful," Ben said finally, his voice low. "You're smarter than most people here, Carter. That's not always a good thing."

With that, he stood, grabbing his coffee and walking away without another word. Isabella watched him go, her thoughts spinning.

Ben's reluctance to answer her questions was infuriating, but it also told her something important: he was scared. And if someone like Ben—calm, collected, and seemingly unflappable—was scared, then she had every reason to be, too.

But she couldn't shake the feeling that she was already in too deep to stop now.

The sun dipped lower in the sky, casting long shadows across the quad as Isabella caught up with Ben outside the library. His usual air of detachment seemed heavier tonight, his hands stuffed deep in his jacket pockets and his gaze fixed on the ground as he walked. She fell into step beside him, her mind still buzzing with their last conversation.

"You know, you're pretty good at warning me off without actually saying anything," she said, her tone light but probing.

Ben glanced at her, one brow arched. "You don't seem like the type to listen to warnings anyway."

"Not when they're vague and cryptic," Isabella replied. "But if you gave me something real to work with, I might actually consider it."

Ben sighed, his steps slowing as they approached the edge of the quad. "What do you want to know, Carter? That people have tried to fight back before? That it didn't end well?"

Her heart skipped a beat. "So, people have resisted?"

Ben stopped walking, turning to face her. His expression was unreadable, but his voice carried an edge of caution. "A few. Not many. And they all had one thing in common."

"What?" Isabella asked, her voice barely above a whisper.

"They underestimated the Syndicate," Ben said simply. "They thought they could outsmart them, expose them, take them down. And they paid for it."

"What happened to them?" Isabella pressed, her curiosity tinged with dread.

Ben hesitated, his gaze flicking to the darkened windows of the library behind her. "Some disappeared, like Harker and Ethan. Others... stayed, but they weren't the same after. It's like they broke something in themselves trying to push back. Their grades slipped, their relationships fell apart. A few even left voluntarily, but not before the Syndicate made sure they'd regret it."

The weight of his words settled over her, heavy and oppressive. She swallowed hard, her mind racing. "Why haven't I heard about any of this?"

"Because no one talks about it," Ben said, his tone flat. "The Syndicate doesn't just punish resistance—they erase it. They make sure the people who fight back become cautionary tales, not inspirations."

"But there must be someone," Isabella insisted, her voice rising slightly. "Someone who's managed to stand up to them and survive."

Ben shook his head, though his expression softened slightly. "If there is, I haven't met them. The Syndicate's power isn't just in what they can do to you—it's in making you believe there's no point in fighting."

Isabella crossed her arms, frustration bubbling beneath the surface. "So, what? We're just supposed to roll over and accept it?"

"That's not what I'm saying," Ben replied, his voice firm. "But if you're going to fight back, you need to be smart about it. Reckless resistance is just another way to hand them exactly what they want."

"Then what's the right way?" Isabella asked, narrowing her eyes. "You talk like you've figured it out, but all you ever do is tell me to keep my head down."

"Because that's the first rule," Ben said sharply. "You can't fight them if they know you're a threat. The moment you draw attention to yourself, you've already lost."

She frowned, her thoughts spinning. "So, what? I just pretend everything's fine while they watch my every move?"

Ben's lips quirked into a bitter smile. "Pretending is half the game, Carter. But the other half is knowing when to act—and when not to."

Isabella fell silent, her gaze dropping to the ground. The idea of resistance intrigued her, but the stakes felt impossibly high. If others had tried and failed, what chance did she have?

Ben must have sensed her doubt because he stepped closer, his tone softening. "Look, I get it. You want to believe you can change things. Maybe you can. But if you go charging in without a plan, you're just going to get yourself hurt—or worse."

She looked up at him, her chest tightening. "Then help me. If you know so much, why won't you help me figure this out?"

Ben hesitated, his jaw tightening. "Because I've seen what happens to the people who try. And I'm not going to stand here and watch you make the same mistakes."

His words stung, but they also lit a spark of determination in her. She wasn't ready to give up, not yet. "I'm not asking you to fight for me," she said, her voice steady. "Just don't stop me from trying."

Ben sighed, running a hand through his hair. "Fine. But if you're going to do this, at least promise me you'll be careful."

"I will," Isabella said, though the fire in her eyes betrayed a recklessness she couldn't suppress.

Ben shook his head, a faint, wry smile tugging at his lips. "You're impossible, you know that?"

She smirked, the tension between them easing slightly. "I've been told."

As they resumed walking, the conversation lingered in the air, unspoken but ever-present. Isabella's mind raced with possibilities, her fear tempered by a growing sense of purpose. She didn't know what resistance would look like yet, but one thing was clear: she wasn't going to let the Syndicate win without a fight.

And for the first time, she thought Ben might not, either.

The sky above Barrington was streaked with shades of gray, the soft drizzle creating a damp chill that clung to the air. Isabella and Ben walked side by side along the winding path toward the dorms, their footsteps muffled by the wet cobblestones. For once, the tension between them seemed to have ebbed, leaving a comfortable silence in its place.

"You're quiet," Ben remarked, glancing sideways at her. His tone was light, but there was an edge of curiosity beneath it.

"Just thinking," Isabella replied, tucking her hands into her jacket pockets. "About everything you said earlier."

"Ah," Ben said with a knowing smirk. "The part where I told you not to be an idiot?"

She shot him a look, her lips twitching into a faint smile despite herself. "The part where you told me there's no point in fighting back."

"I didn't say there's no point," Ben corrected. "I said it's dangerous. Big difference."

"Right," Isabella said, her voice dripping with sarcasm. "Totally reassuring."

Ben chuckled softly, but the sound faded as his expression grew more serious. "Look, Carter, I'm not trying to scare you off. I just don't want to see you get hurt."

The sincerity in his voice caught her off guard, and she looked up at him, surprised. "Why do you care so much?"

Ben hesitated, his gaze flicking to the path ahead. "Because I've seen this place chew people up and spit them out. And you're... different."

"Different how?" Isabella asked, tilting her head.

Ben let out a slow breath, running a hand through his hair. "You're not like the others. Most people here either don't see what's going on, or they're too afraid to do anything about it. But you—you actually care. You want to understand."

"Of course I do," Isabella said. "How else am I supposed to survive?"

"That's the thing," Ben said, stopping and turning to face her. "Most people survive by not understanding. By not asking questions. You're not wired that way."

Isabella studied him for a moment, her chest tightening. "And that's a bad thing?"

"No," Ben admitted, his voice softening. "It's just... risky."

They stood in silence for a moment, the drizzle pattering against their jackets. Finally, Ben reached out and gently grabbed her elbow, steering her off the main path and toward a small, sheltered alcove beneath the arch of an old stone building.

"You're freezing," he said, shrugging off his jacket and draping it over her shoulders before she could protest.

"I'm fine," Isabella said, though the warmth of the jacket was welcome.

"Humor me," Ben replied, leaning against the wall and crossing his arms. "You've got that stubborn look again."

"Stubborn?" Isabella repeated, raising an eyebrow.

"Yeah," Ben said with a faint smirk. "The one that says you're about to do something reckless."

"I'm not reckless," Isabella insisted, though her tone lacked conviction.

Ben's smirk faded, replaced by a softer expression. "I mean it, Carter. Whatever you're planning, just... don't go it alone. Promise me."

The seriousness in his voice made her pause. "Why do you care so much?" she asked again, her voice quieter this time.

Ben hesitated, his gaze dropping to the ground. "Because I've seen what happens to people who try to take this place on by themselves. And I don't want that to happen to you."

Isabella's chest tightened at the vulnerability in his words. She wasn't used to seeing this side of him—the one that wasn't sarcastic or guarded, but genuinely concerned.

"Thanks," she said softly, pulling the jacket tighter around her shoulders. "For looking out for me."

Ben shrugged, his usual smirk returning. "Don't mention it. Just don't make me regret it."

The faint sound of laughter drifted from a nearby building, breaking the moment. Isabella glanced toward the sound, then back at Ben, her curiosity gnawing at her.

"Ben," she said carefully, "why are you still here? If you've seen what this place can do, why stay?"

His smirk faltered, and for a moment, she thought he wouldn't answer. But then he sighed, running a hand through his hair again. "Because leaving isn't the same as escaping. Barrington doesn't let you go, not really. If you're here, you're part of it. And if you leave... they make sure you never forget it."

The weight of his words settled over her like a heavy blanket. She wanted to press him further, to ask what he meant, but the look in his eyes stopped her.

Instead, she nodded, her determination hardening. "Then I guess I'll have to figure out how to survive without giving up who I am."

Ben smiled faintly, though it didn't reach his eyes. "Good luck with that. Just remember—you've got someone in your corner."

The words warmed her, even as they left her with more questions than answers. As they walked back toward the dorms, Isabella couldn't shake the feeling that Ben's concern ran deeper than he was letting on. And for the first time, she wondered if his own survival had come at a cost she couldn't yet imagine.

Chapter 8
Chains of Influence

The office was dimly lit, the only illumination coming from the faint glow of a brass desk lamp and the muted sunlight filtering through heavy curtains. Isabella sat stiffly in the chair across from Thorne's desk, her fingers gripping the edges of her notebook. The air in the room felt heavy, as if the walls themselves were listening.

"Miss Carter," Thorne began, leaning back in his leather chair. His voice was smooth, each word deliberate. "I must say, your performance has been... exemplary."

"Thank you, Professor," Isabella replied cautiously, unsure of where the conversation was headed.

Thorne steepled his fingers, his piercing gaze fixed on her. "It's rare for a first-year student to display such a deep understanding of Barrington's academic rigors. Rarer still to exhibit the intuition you've demonstrated."

Isabella shifted uncomfortably. "I'm just trying to keep up."

Thorne smiled faintly, though there was no warmth in it. "Don't undervalue yourself. Keeping up, as you put it, is not what you're doing. You're excelling. Outpacing, even."

She wasn't sure how to respond, so she nodded, her grip on her notebook tightening.

"However," Thorne continued, his tone softening as he leaned forward, "excellence comes with expectations."

"Expectations?" Isabella echoed, her pulse quickening.

"Indeed." Thorne opened a folder on his desk, sliding a single sheet of paper across to her. It was a list of names, most of them unfamiliar. At the top, however, was the name **William Harker**—a detail that sent a shiver down her spine.

"I'd like you to review this," Thorne said, his voice casual. "Nothing too strenuous, of course. Just a bit of additional research. Connections, histories, patterns. You're quite adept at uncovering those, aren't you?"

Isabella stared at the list, her chest tightening. "What kind of research?"

"Consider it an exercise in observation," Thorne said, his tone light but calculated. "Look into these individuals—where they've been, what they've achieved, and how they've contributed to Barrington. We'll discuss your findings at our next meeting."

She looked up, meeting his gaze. "Is this related to my coursework?"

Thorne smiled faintly, though it didn't reach his eyes. "Not directly. But understanding Barrington's network is as crucial as excelling in its academics. Think of this as an opportunity to broaden your perspective."

"I'm not sure I understand the purpose," Isabella said cautiously.

"The purpose," Thorne said, his tone sharpening, "is to see how well you follow instructions. Loyalty, Miss Carter, is not just about obedience. It's about trust. Initiative. Proving that you can be relied upon, even when the task seems... unconventional."

Isabella's stomach churned. She glanced back at the list, the names blurring slightly as her mind raced. "What happens if I don't find anything?"

Thorne's smile returned, though it carried a hint of warning. "You'll find something. You're resourceful. And resourcefulness, Miss Carter, is a quality we value highly at Barrington."

The subtle emphasis on "we" sent a chill down her spine. She swallowed hard, forcing herself to stay composed. "I'll do my best."

"I have no doubt you will," Thorne said, leaning back again. "But remember—this is more than an academic exercise. It's an opportunity to demonstrate your alignment with Barrington's values."

"Alignment?" Isabella asked, the word sticking in her throat.

"Loyalty," Thorne clarified, his gaze unwavering. "And discretion."

Isabella nodded slowly, her mind spinning with questions she didn't dare ask. She stood, clutching the paper tightly in one hand and her notebook in the other.

"Thank you, Professor," she said, her voice steadier than she felt.

Thorne rose as well, his smile lingering. "I'll look forward to your insights. And Miss Carter—remember, we notice those who go above and beyond."

As she left the office, the door clicking shut behind her, Isabella's chest felt tight. The list in her hand felt heavier with every step she took. The names stared back at her, each one a mystery she was now expected to unravel.

This wasn't just a task. It was a test. And failure, she realized, wasn't an option. But the bigger question loomed: What would success mean?

And how much of herself was she willing to sacrifice to find out?

Isabella stood in front of Professor Thorne's desk, her arms crossed tightly over her chest. The faint ticking of the clock on the wall seemed unnaturally loud in the tense silence of the room. Thorne, seated comfortably in his high-backed chair, studied her with the calm, calculating gaze that always made her feel like she was under a microscope.

"You're not answering my question," Isabella said, her voice firmer than she felt.

Thorne smiled faintly, steepling his fingers. "On the contrary, Miss Carter, I've been answering it all along. You simply haven't been listening."

"I've been listening," Isabella replied, her tone sharp. "You keep talking about loyalty and initiative, but none of that explains why you've decided to single me out."

Thorne leaned back, his eyes narrowing slightly. "You're not being singled out. You're being given an opportunity."

"An opportunity to what?" Isabella pressed, stepping closer. "To prove myself? To play some game I don't even understand? If this is about my scholarship—"

"This is not about your scholarship," Thorne interrupted smoothly, his tone low but commanding. "This is about potential, Miss Carter. Yours."

Isabella's chest tightened. "What does that even mean?"

"It means you have a gift," Thorne said, rising slowly from his chair. He circled the desk, his presence both imposing and oddly casual. "A way of seeing things that others don't. That others can't."

She stiffened, her thoughts darting to the puzzle she'd solved so effortlessly, the moments of clarity that seemed to strike out of nowhere. "You don't even know me."

Thorne chuckled, the sound soft and unsettling. "Don't I? Do you think we bring students like you here without knowing exactly what we're getting?"

Her stomach twisted. "So, what? You've been watching me this whole time?"

"We watch everyone, Miss Carter," Thorne said, his tone maddeningly calm. "But some stand out more than others. And you... well, you've been standing out since the moment you arrived."

Isabella's fingers curled into fists at her sides. "If you're trying to scare me, it's not working."

"Good," Thorne said, his smile sharp. "Fear is a distraction. What I want from you is focus."

"Focus on what?" Isabella asked, her frustration bubbling to the surface. "I didn't come here to be some kind of experiment."

Thorne's gaze darkened, though his tone remained measured. "Experiment? Hardly. You're here because you belong here. Because you have the potential to achieve greatness—if you're willing to embrace it."

"What does that mean?" Isabella demanded. "What are you not telling me?"

Thorne paused, as though weighing how much to reveal. Finally, he stepped closer, his voice dropping to a near whisper.

"Do you think Barrington is like other schools? That our scholarships, our resources, our connections are offered without expectation?"

Isabella's breath caught, her pulse quickening. "What expectations?"

Thorne smiled faintly. "Alignment, Miss Carter. Loyalty to something greater than yourself. The Syndicate recognizes those with the potential to make a difference, to contribute to the system that sustains us all."

"The Syndicate," Isabella said, the name feeling heavy in her mouth. "What does that have to do with me?"

Thorne tilted his head slightly, his gaze piercing. "Everything. They see what I see—a mind capable of extraordinary things. But with extraordinary potential comes extraordinary scrutiny."

Isabella stepped back, her throat tightening. "You're saying they're watching me?"

"Of course," Thorne said simply. "They're watching everyone. But you, Miss Carter, are particularly interesting. The question is—how will you use that interest to your advantage?"

She stared at him, her mind spinning. "What if I don't want their interest?"

Thorne's expression didn't change, but there was a flicker of something—amusement, perhaps—in his eyes. "You don't have a choice. Not anymore."

The words sent a chill down her spine, and she swallowed hard, struggling to keep her composure. "What exactly do you want from me?"

"What I want," Thorne said, his voice softening, "is for you to rise to the occasion. To prove that my faith in you is not misplaced. To show the Syndicate that you're worth their investment."

"And if I don't?" Isabella asked, her voice trembling slightly.

Thorne smiled again, but this time it felt colder, more calculated. "Let's not dwell on hypotheticals, shall we? I prefer to focus on what's possible. And you, Miss Carter, are full of possibilities."

The room fell silent, the weight of his words pressing down on her like a heavy fog. She wanted to argue, to demand answers, but the intensity of his gaze left her feeling exposed, vulnerable.

Finally, Thorne stepped back, his demeanor shifting once more to casual authority. "That will be all for now. I trust you'll continue to exceed expectations."

Isabella nodded stiffly, her thoughts churning as she turned to leave. As the door closed behind her, her chest tightened with a mix of fear and determination.

Thorne's manipulations were growing clearer, but so was the truth: if the Syndicate had set their sights on her, she would have to navigate their game carefully—or risk losing herself entirely.

The library was unusually empty that evening, the quiet punctuated only by the faint hum of fluorescent lights and the occasional shuffle of books being reshelved. Isabella sat at a table in the back corner, her notebook open to the list Thorne had given her. The names stared back at her, each one a mystery she hadn't yet begun to unravel.

"Trouble?" a voice asked, pulling her from her thoughts.

She looked up to see Chloe, a fellow scholarship student, standing by her table. Chloe was rarely seen without a book in hand, her sharp eyes always seeming to miss nothing. Tonight, she looked more cautious than usual, glancing over her shoulder before sliding into the chair across from Isabella.

"What do you want?" Isabella asked, trying to keep her tone neutral.

Chloe's gaze dropped to the notebook in front of her. "You're working on something for Thorne, aren't you?"

Isabella stiffened. "Why would you think that?"

"Because I've been there," Chloe said simply, folding her arms on the table. "He gave you a task, didn't he? Something that seems straightforward but doesn't feel right?"

Isabella hesitated, then nodded slowly. "How do you know?"

Chloe sighed, leaning back in her chair. "Because he does this every year. Picks one or two of us, dangles some carrot about potential or opportunity, and then uses us to do his dirty work."

"What kind of dirty work?" Isabella asked, her voice lowering.

Chloe's lips pressed into a thin line. "Research. Reports. Little things that seem harmless until you realize what he's really after."

"And what's that?" Isabella asked, her pulse quickening.

Chloe hesitated, her gaze flicking around the library again before she leaned in closer. "Control. Thorne doesn't just want loyalty—he wants leverage. And the more you give him, the more he has to use against you."

Isabella frowned, glancing down at the list again. "But this… it's just research. How bad could it be?"

"That's what I thought, too," Chloe said bitterly. "But it's never just research. He's testing you, Isabella. Seeing how far you're willing to go, how much you're willing to give. And once you cross a line, you can't go back."

The weight of her words settled over Isabella like a heavy fog. "What happened to you?"

Chloe hesitated, her fingers tracing invisible patterns on the table. "He asked me to look into another student—a senior who was on a scholarship like us. Told me it was for some kind of mentorship program. I believed him."

"And?" Isabella prompted.

"And I found out later that the student was under investigation by the Syndicate," Chloe said, her voice tight. "Thorne used my research to build a case against them. I don't know what they did or why, but they were expelled within a week. No explanation. No chance to defend themselves."

Isabella's stomach churned. "Did you tell anyone?"

"Who was I supposed to tell?" Chloe asked, her voice rising slightly. "The administration? They're in on it. The professors? Half of them are probably part of the Syndicate. And the other half are too scared to do anything."

Isabella leaned back in her chair, her mind racing. "Why are you telling me this?"

"Because you're new," Chloe said, her tone softening. "And I can see where this is going. Thorne's not just testing your skills—he's testing your loyalty. And if you're not careful, you'll end up just like me."

"And how's that?" Isabella asked, her voice tinged with bitterness.

Chloe's gaze hardened. "Used. Compromised. And too scared to fight back."

The silence between them was heavy, the library's quiet suddenly feeling oppressive. Isabella closed her notebook, her hands trembling slightly. "So, what do I do?"

Chloe sighed, standing up and grabbing her bag. "That's up to you. But if you want my advice—don't give Thorne more than you have to. He's good at making it seem like you're the one in control, but trust me, you're not."

Isabella watched her walk away, the sound of her footsteps fading into the distance. Alone again, she looked back at the list, her resolve hardening. Chloe's warning only deepened her mistrust of Thorne, but it also left her with more questions than answers.

If Thorne was playing a game, she needed to figure out the rules—and fast. But as she sat there, staring at the names on the page, one thought stood out above the rest: how much longer could she keep playing without losing herself?

The air in Professor Thorne's office felt colder than usual, the dim light from the desk lamp casting long shadows across the room. Isabella sat stiffly in the chair, her hands folded tightly in her lap as Thorne leaned back in his chair, studying her with an expression that was equal parts calculated and amused.

"You've been doing well so far, Miss Carter," he began, his voice smooth and deliberate. "Your insights have been... enlightening."

"Thank you," Isabella replied cautiously, unsure if the compliment was genuine or another manipulation.

Thorne's faint smile didn't waver. "Which is why I'm confident you're ready for a more focused task."

He opened a file folder on his desk and slid a single sheet of paper toward her. Isabella hesitated before picking it up. The name at the top of the page caught her eye immediately: **Adam Sinclair.**

"Who is he?" she asked, her voice steady despite the unease twisting in her stomach.

"Mr. Sinclair is one of our more promising students," Thorne replied, his tone casual. "A natural leader, highly intelligent, and well-connected. But even the most promising individuals occasionally require... oversight."

"Oversight?" Isabella repeated, frowning.

Thorne leaned forward slightly, his gaze sharpening. "I'd like you to observe him. Pay attention to his habits, his interactions, his priorities. Take note of anything unusual."

Isabella's grip on the paper tightened. "Why me?"

"Because you have a talent for seeing what others miss," Thorne said smoothly. "And because this is an opportunity for you to prove your reliability."

She swallowed hard, her gaze dropping to the paper. The task felt invasive, almost voyeuristic. "What am I supposed to be looking for?"

"Patterns," Thorne said simply. "Consistency—or the lack thereof. Adam is an asset to Barrington, but assets must be managed carefully. Your observations will help ensure he remains on the right path."

Isabella hesitated. "And if he's not?"

"That's not your concern," Thorne said, his tone sharpening slightly. "Your job is to observe and report. Nothing more."

The finality in his voice left no room for argument. Isabella glanced back at the paper, a growing sense of dread settling over her. She wanted to refuse, to push back against the task, but the look in Thorne's eyes stopped her. He wasn't just testing her abilities—he was testing her loyalty.

"I'll do it," she said finally, though the words felt like a betrayal of her own values.

Thorne's smile returned, faint and calculating. "Good. I knew I could count on you."

She stood, clutching the paper tightly as she turned to leave. But as her hand reached for the door, Thorne's voice stopped her.

"Miss Carter."

She turned back, her heart pounding. "Yes, Professor?"

"This task is about more than observation," Thorne said, his gaze unyielding. "It's about trust. Prove that you can handle this, and there will be more opportunities for you in the future."

"And if I can't?" Isabella asked, her voice barely above a whisper.

Thorne's smile didn't falter, but his tone carried a subtle warning. "I would advise against failure. It rarely ends well."

The weight of his words hung in the air as Isabella stepped out of the office, the door clicking shut behind her. She stood in the hallway for a long moment, staring down at the paper in her hand.

The assignment felt wrong, invasive, and manipulative, but she couldn't deny the subtle thrill of being trusted with something important. That thrill was quickly overshadowed by the realization of what was at stake.

Thorne had framed this as an opportunity, but it felt more like a trap. And as much as she wanted to resist, she knew she couldn't afford to fail.

Tucking the paper into her notebook, she headed toward the dorms, her thoughts churning with questions she couldn't yet answer. Who was Adam Sinclair, really? And why did Thorne care so much about him?

Most importantly, how much of herself was Isabella willing to compromise to prove her worth?

Chapter 9
The Unseen Strings

The common room buzzed with subdued chatter, students lounging on couches or flipping through textbooks at the scattered tables. The familiar hum of campus life should have felt comforting, but Isabella couldn't shake the gnawing unease in her chest. Her eyes darted around the room, scanning for something she couldn't quite name.

She paused by the entrance, her gaze catching on the oversized clock mounted above the doorway. At first glance, it seemed ordinary—bronze hands ticking steadily across a polished black face—but something about it felt... off. Narrowing her eyes, Isabella stepped closer, pretending to adjust the strap of her bag as she examined the clock more closely.

The faint glint of a lens caught her eye. Tiny, almost invisible, but unmistakable.

Her breath hitched, and she stepped back quickly, bumping into Rachel, who was carrying a cup of coffee. The liquid sloshed over the rim, a few drops splattering onto the floor.

"Watch it!" Rachel snapped before recognizing Isabella. Her annoyed expression softened into concern. "What's your deal?"

"Sorry," Isabella muttered, barely hearing her. Her gaze flicked back to the clock.

Rachel followed her line of sight and frowned. "What are you looking at?"

"The clock," Isabella whispered, her voice tight. "There's a camera in it."

Rachel's eyes widened briefly before she schooled her expression. "You sure?"

"Positive," Isabella replied, her heart pounding. "It's the same as the one in the chandelier. I can see the lens."

Rachel grabbed her arm, steering her toward the farthest corner of the room. "Okay, lower your voice," she said, her tone hushed. "You want to give yourself away?"

"Give myself away to who?" Isabella hissed. "It's not like they don't already know I'm here."

"That doesn't mean you need to confirm it," Rachel shot back, her grip tightening. "You think they're just watching for fun? They're waiting for you to slip up."

Isabella wrenched her arm free, her frustration bubbling over. "And what happens if I do? What's the worst they can do to me?"

Rachel leaned in, her expression dark. "You don't want to find out."

The words sent a chill down Isabella's spine. She looked around the room again, her paranoia growing with every passing second. The cameras could be anywhere. Everywhere. How many had she missed? How often had they been watching her without her even realizing it?

"I can't live like this," Isabella said, her voice trembling. "It's like... like I'm being suffocated."

Rachel's expression softened, and she sighed. "I get it. I do. But freaking out isn't going to help. You have to stay calm, keep your head down."

"Easy for you to say," Isabella snapped. "You're not the one they've got under a microscope."

Rachel raised an eyebrow. "You think I'm not? They're watching all of us, Carter. The difference is, I'm not giving them a reason to look closer."

Isabella opened her mouth to argue but stopped herself. Rachel was right. Losing control wasn't going to help her, but the thought of doing nothing felt unbearable. She closed her eyes, taking a slow, deep breath.

"Fine," she said finally. "I'll stay calm. But I'm not going to ignore this."

Rachel shook her head. "You're going to get yourself in trouble."

"Maybe," Isabella said, her voice firm. "But I'm not going to let them scare me into silence."

Rachel stared at her for a long moment before sighing again. "Just... be careful, okay? They're not playing games."

"I know," Isabella said, though the words felt hollow.

She turned away, her gaze drifting back to the clock as Rachel left the room. The knowledge of the camera burned in her mind, a constant reminder of the unseen eyes watching her every move. She could feel the weight of their scrutiny, the suffocating pressure of being observed.

As she headed toward the stairs, her thoughts churned. If the cameras were in the common area, where else were they? Her dorm room? The library? The quad?

The questions clawed at her, each one more disturbing than the last. She knew one thing for certain: she couldn't trust anything—or anyone—at Barrington.

And she wasn't sure how much longer she could endure it.

The courtyard buzzed with an uneasy energy, students gathering in small groups under the gray afternoon sky. Whispers floated through the crowd, too low to catch but filled with tension. Isabella stood near the back, her arms crossed as she scanned the faces around her. Everyone seemed to know something was about to happen, but no one dared to say it aloud.

A sharp, deliberate voice cut through the murmur. "Attention, students."

The crowd shifted, heads turning toward the stone steps leading to the administration building. There, framed by the imposing columns, stood Dean Harrington. Beside him was a boy Isabella recognized—Jacob Ellison, a fellow scholarship student. He looked pale and shaken, his hands clasped tightly in front of him as he stared at the ground.

"Jacob Ellison has violated the rules of this institution," Dean Harrington continued, his voice carrying effortlessly over the courtyard. "He accessed a restricted area without permission, disregarding clear directives."

Isabella's stomach dropped. Jacob? He was quiet, studious, the last person she'd expect to break a rule. She glanced at Rachel, who stood a few feet away, her expression carefully neutral.

"Why would he do that?" Isabella whispered, leaning toward her.

Rachel didn't look at her. "I don't know, and I don't want to know."

The Dean's voice rose, silencing the murmurs. "Barrington is a place of opportunity, but it is also a place of discipline. Rules exist for a reason. Disobedience will not be tolerated."

Jacob flinched at the words, his shoulders hunching slightly. Isabella felt a pang of sympathy and fear. Whatever was happening, it wasn't just about punishment—it was about making an example of him.

"Jacob," Dean Harrington said, turning to the boy. "Do you have anything to say for yourself?"

Jacob hesitated, his eyes darting toward the crowd. When he finally spoke, his voice was barely audible. "I didn't mean to—"

"Speak up," the Dean snapped.

"I didn't mean to disobey," Jacob said louder, his voice trembling. "I didn't know the area was restricted."

"That is not an excuse," Harrington said coldly. "You ignored clear signage and security protocols. Your actions were reckless and disrespectful."

Isabella clenched her fists, her heart pounding. The Dean's words felt rehearsed, calculated to instill fear in everyone watching. This wasn't just about Jacob—it was a message to the entire student body.

"Effective immediately," Harrington continued, "Jacob's access to certain privileges will be revoked. He will be confined to his dorm outside of class hours, and his scholarship will be subject to review."

A ripple of shock passed through the crowd. Isabella's breath caught. Losing a scholarship was tantamount to expulsion for someone like Jacob. The stakes couldn't be clearer.

"Let this serve as a reminder to all of you," the Dean said, his gaze sweeping over the students. "Barrington expects excellence, discipline, and loyalty. Those who fail to uphold these values will face the consequences."

With that, he turned and walked back into the building, leaving Jacob standing alone on the steps. The crowd began to disperse, the whispers growing louder as students hurried away.

Isabella stayed rooted to the spot, her mind racing. She wanted to go to Jacob, to offer some kind of support, but Rachel grabbed her arm before she could move.

"Don't," Rachel said firmly.

"He needs help," Isabella protested, her voice low.

"There's nothing you can do for him," Rachel said, her tone clipped. "If you get involved, you'll just paint a target on your back."

Isabella yanked her arm free, glaring at her. "You're just going to stand by and do nothing?"

"That's exactly what I'm going to do," Rachel said. "And so are you. Unless you want to end up like him."

The warning in her voice was clear, but it only made Isabella's anger burn hotter. "This isn't right."

"It doesn't matter if it's right," Rachel said sharply. "It's how things work here. The Syndicate doesn't care about fairness.

They care about control. And today, they made sure we all know it."

Isabella looked back at Jacob, who was being ushered away by two faculty members. His head was bowed, his shoulders slumped, as though the weight of the punishment had already crushed him.

Rachel stepped closer, her voice softening slightly. "I know you hate this. So do I. But the best thing you can do is keep your head down and stay out of it."

Isabella didn't respond. She couldn't. The anger and fear swirling inside her were too overwhelming. She turned and walked away, her thoughts a chaotic storm.

The Syndicate's message had been clear: they were always watching, and stepping out of line came at a cost. But as much as the display had shaken her, it also solidified something deep within her. She couldn't ignore this. Not anymore.

As she reached the edge of the courtyard, she glanced back one last time. The steps were empty now, but the memory of Jacob's punishment lingered, a stark reminder of the dangers she faced.

The Syndicate had shown their power. Now, it was up to Isabella to decide what to do about it.

The sun had dipped below the horizon, casting the campus in a dim, bluish glow. Isabella sat on the low stone wall outside the library, the brisk evening air nipping at her cheeks. She spotted Ben approaching from across the quad, his hands shoved deep into his jacket pockets and his stride purposeful.

"I heard about Jacob," he said as he reached her, his voice low.

"Everyone has," Isabella replied, pulling her jacket tighter around her. "They made sure of that."

Ben leaned against the wall beside her, his expression dark. "That's how they work. Public discipline is a tool, just like surveillance. They don't just punish—they make examples."

"Do you think he deserved it?" Isabella asked, glancing at him.

Ben's jaw tightened. "It's not about deserving. It's about control. Jacob made a mistake, sure, but the punishment wasn't about him. It was about keeping the rest of us in line."

Isabella frowned, her thoughts spinning. "You talk like you've been through this before."

Ben hesitated, his gaze fixed on the ground. "I have."

"What happened?" she asked, turning to face him.

He sighed, dragging a hand through his hair. "First year. I was still figuring out how things worked here, didn't know where the lines were. I missed a curfew once—just by a few minutes—and didn't think much of it. The next day, I found a note in my dorm."

"A note?" Isabella echoed, her stomach tightening.

Ben nodded. "Just one sentence: 'Punctuality is a reflection of discipline.' No name, no signature. But the message was clear. I was being watched."

"That's it?" Isabella asked, her voice tinged with disbelief. "A warning?"

"At first, yeah," Ben said, his tone grim. "But then it escalated. A few weeks later, I was in the library working on an assignment. I got a little too curious about a restricted section—didn't even go in, just lingered near the door too long. The next day, I was summoned to Thorne's office."

Isabella's breath caught. "What did he say?"

Ben let out a bitter laugh. "He didn't have to say much. Just made a few comments about the importance of 'boundaries' and how rules are in place to protect us. It was all very polite, very vague. But the message was the same as the note: they're watching, and they don't like curiosity."

"That's ridiculous," Isabella said, anger bubbling in her chest.

"It's Barrington," Ben replied simply. "They don't care about fairness or logic. They care about maintaining control. And they'll use whatever means necessary to do it."

She stared at him, her thoughts racing. "So, what did you do?"

"What do you think?" Ben asked, his tone sharper now. "I kept my head down. Stopped asking questions. Stayed out of places I wasn't supposed to be. And it worked—for the most part. But I still get reminders every now and then."

"Reminders?" Isabella asked, frowning.

Ben nodded. "Little things. A comment from a professor that's just specific enough to feel personal. An email that doesn't say much but says enough. They let you know you're still on their radar, even if you haven't done anything wrong lately."

Isabella shivered, the weight of his words settling over her. "But why? What's the point of all this surveillance and discipline? It feels... excessive."

Ben looked at her, his expression softer now. "Because fear is the most effective way to keep people in line. If you're always worried about being watched, about slipping up, you're not thinking about resisting. You're not thinking about anything but survival."

The silence between them stretched, heavy and oppressive. Isabella stared at the cobblestones beneath her feet, her mind spinning with everything Ben had said.

"Is that what you think I should do?" she asked finally. "Keep my head down, stop asking questions?"

Ben hesitated, his gaze flicking toward the shadowy outline of the administration building in the distance. "I think you should be careful," he said eventually. "You're smart, Carter. Smarter than most people here. But that makes you a threat. And threats don't last long at Barrington."

"I don't want to just survive," Isabella said, her voice trembling slightly. "I can't live like that."

Ben sighed, turning to face her fully. "Then be smart about how you push back. Don't make the same mistakes I did. They're watching you, just like they're watching me. Don't give them a reason to tighten the leash."

Isabella met his gaze, the weight of his warning sinking in. "I'll be careful."

"You'd better," Ben said, his voice soft but firm. "Because once they decide you're a problem, there's no going back."

As he walked away, his words echoed in her mind, each one laced with a truth she couldn't ignore. The Syndicate's surveillance wasn't just a tool—it was a weapon. And the line between survival and subjugation was thinner than she'd ever realized.

For the first time, Isabella wondered if she was already too far over it.

The office felt colder than usual, the faint hum of the overhead light the only sound as Isabella stepped inside. Thorne sat behind his desk, his fingers steepled and his gaze fixed on her as if he had been waiting for this moment all day. She closed the door behind her, feeling the weight of his attention settle over her like a heavy blanket.

"Miss Carter," he said, his voice smooth and deliberate. "Thank you for coming."

"You didn't leave me much of a choice," Isabella replied, trying to keep her voice steady. The curt summons to his office had been anything but optional.

Thorne's lips curved into a faint smile, though there was no warmth in it. "You're a bright young woman, so I'll assume you understand the importance of this conversation. Let's dispense with pleasantries, shall we?"

Isabella nodded, her chest tightening. She didn't trust herself to speak.

Thorne leaned forward slightly, his eyes narrowing. "I've been hearing... things. Questions being asked. Concerns being raised. About cameras, surveillance, and the like."

Her heart skipped a beat, but she forced herself to remain calm. "I thought students were encouraged to ask questions," she said, careful to keep her tone neutral.

"Curiosity is a valuable trait," Thorne replied smoothly. "But only when it's directed appropriately. Barrington thrives on structure, Miss Carter. And that structure depends on trust—trust in the system, trust in those who oversee it."

"Isn't trust a two-way street?" Isabella asked before she could stop herself.

Thorne's smile faltered, his gaze sharpening. "Trust is earned, Miss Carter. And it is maintained by understanding one's place within the system."

Isabella shifted uneasily, her mind racing. "I wasn't trying to undermine anything," she said carefully. "I was just... curious."

"Curiosity can be dangerous," Thorne said, his voice dropping. "Especially when it leads to... misunderstandings."

"What misunderstandings?" Isabella asked, her pulse quickening.

Thorne rose from his chair, circling the desk to stand a few feet from her. His presence felt overwhelming, his gaze unrelenting. "The kind that suggest a lack of alignment. A misstep here, a misplaced word there—it can give the wrong impression."

"I'm not trying to give any impression," Isabella said quickly, her voice trembling despite her efforts to stay composed.

"Good," Thorne said, his tone softening slightly. "Because this institution has a vested interest in its students' success. But that success depends on their ability to follow the rules, to trust in the system, and to avoid unnecessary… distractions."

The unspoken threat hung in the air, heavy and oppressive. Isabella clenched her fists, her nails digging into her palms as she forced herself to meet his gaze. "I understand."

"Do you?" Thorne asked, tilting his head slightly. "Because understanding is the cornerstone of loyalty. And loyalty, Miss Carter, is not just about obedience. It's about conviction. Alignment."

The word echoed in her mind, each syllable laced with warning. She swallowed hard, nodding slowly. "I understand," she repeated.

"Good," Thorne said, his smile returning, though it felt more like a mask than an expression. "I knew you would. You've always been one of our most promising students."

He stepped back, gesturing toward the door. "That will be all for now. But remember, Miss Carter—loyalty isn't just about what you do. It's about what you think. And here at Barrington, we value clarity of thought."

Isabella nodded once more, her heart pounding as she turned to leave. The weight of his gaze followed her as she stepped into the hallway, the door clicking shut behind her.

She paused, leaning against the wall as she tried to steady her breathing. Thorne's words replayed in her mind, each one a reminder of the delicate line she was walking. The Syndicate wasn't just watching her—they were evaluating her, testing her every move.

And she couldn't afford to fail.

As she walked back to her dorm, the cameras she passed felt more oppressive than ever, their silent presence a constant reminder of the eyes that never stopped watching. Thorne's veiled threats had solidified one thing in her mind: at Barrington, there was no such thing as privacy.

And no room for mistakes.

Chapter 10
Testing the Boundaries

The library was quieter than usual, the rows of desks sparsely populated with students hunched over textbooks and laptops. Isabella sat near the back, her notebook open to a half-finished essay, the assigned names from Thorne's list buried under a stack of untouched papers at the corner of the desk.

Her pen moved steadily across the page, each word a small victory. For the first time in weeks, she felt a flicker of control. By deliberately ignoring Thorne's task, she was carving out a space for herself, a moment free from the suffocating expectations of the Syndicate.

"Carter," a voice interrupted, pulling her from her focus.

She looked up to see Ben standing on the other side of the desk, his jacket slung over one shoulder. His sharp eyes scanned the papers in front of her before meeting hers. "You look busy."

"Trying to be," she replied, gesturing to the chair across from her. "Sit, if you want."

Ben slid into the seat, setting his jacket on the back of the chair. "What's with the fortress?" he asked, nodding toward the stack of papers shielding the edge of the desk.

"Just keeping things organized," Isabella said evasively, turning back to her notebook.

He raised an eyebrow but didn't press further. "How's the assignment going?"

"What assignment?" she asked lightly, though her heart skipped a beat.

"The one Thorne gave you," Ben said, his tone casual but his gaze sharp.

She hesitated, her pen pausing mid-sentence. "I haven't started it yet."

Ben leaned back, crossing his arms. "You haven't started it, or you're not planning to?"

"Does it matter?" Isabella asked, her voice soft but firm.

"It does if you're trying to get yourself noticed," Ben said, lowering his voice.

She closed her notebook, leaning forward slightly. "I'm not trying to get noticed. I'm trying to focus on what I actually came here to do—learn."

"And you think ignoring Thorne is the way to do that?" Ben asked, his tone edged with caution.

"I think Thorne doesn't own me," Isabella replied, her voice steady despite the flicker of fear in her chest. "If he has a problem with that, he can tell me himself."

Ben studied her for a moment, his expression unreadable. "You're playing a dangerous game, Carter."

"I'm not playing a game," she shot back. "I'm just tired of being treated like a pawn."

His lips quirked into a faint smile. "Good luck convincing Thorne of that."

Isabella looked away, her resolve hardening. "Maybe he needs to learn he doesn't get to control everything."

Ben sighed, leaning forward to rest his elbows on the table. "Look, I get it. Pushing back feels good. But you need to pick your battles. Thorne isn't the kind of person who lets things slide."

"Then let him come after me," Isabella said, her voice dropping to a near whisper. "I'm not going to spend the rest of my time here jumping every time he says so."

Ben shook his head, though there was a glimmer of something—admiration, perhaps—in his expression. "You've got guts, I'll give you that. Just make sure they don't get you in trouble you can't get out of."

"I'll be fine," Isabella said, though the words felt more like a wish than a promise.

Ben leaned back again, his gaze lingering on her for a moment before he stood. "If you need a lifeline, you know where to find me."

She nodded, watching as he walked away, his presence leaving a strange void in its wake.

As the library settled back into its usual quiet, Isabella turned her attention to the untouched papers on the desk. She knew Ben was right—ignoring Thorne's task was risky, and the consequences could be severe. But for now, the simple act of rebellion gave her a small sense of power, a reminder that she wasn't entirely under their control.

The cameras might be watching. Thorne might be waiting. But for this moment, Isabella felt like herself again.

And she wasn't ready to let that go.

The library's labyrinth of bookshelves grew quieter as Isabella followed Ben deeper into its shadows. The soft glow of the overhead lights barely reached the rows they navigated, and the muffled rustle of pages and faint whispers of other students faded behind them.

"Where are we going?" Isabella whispered, her voice low to match the stillness around them.

"You'll see," Ben replied, glancing back with a small, cryptic smile. He carried his jacket slung over one shoulder, his pace deliberate as he guided her through a series of narrow aisles.

"This place is starting to feel like a maze," Isabella muttered, glancing at the endless rows of books towering above her.

"That's part of its charm," Ben said. "And part of the reason no one bothers coming back here. It's too much effort to find anything."

Finally, they reached the end of a row where an old wooden ladder leaned against the shelf. Ben gestured toward it. "After you."

Isabella raised an eyebrow. "A ladder? What are we, burglars?"

He smirked, stepping aside to let her pass. "You'll thank me later."

Rolling her eyes, Isabella began to climb, the rungs creaking slightly under her weight. She reached the top and stepped onto a narrow landing hidden behind the topmost shelf. A low alcove, barely large enough for two people to sit comfortably, stretched out before her, lined with cushions that looked like they hadn't been moved in years.

"What is this?" she asked, crouching as Ben joined her.

"Sanctuary," he said simply, settling into one of the cushions and stretching out his legs. "No cameras, no microphones, no one looking over your shoulder. It's the only place in this whole school where you can actually breathe."

Isabella sat down slowly, her fingers brushing over the worn fabric of the cushions. "How do you know there aren't cameras?"

"I've checked," Ben said, his tone matter-of-fact. "Trust me, if they were monitoring this spot, I'd have been caught years ago."

She gave him a skeptical look. "Years?"

"First-year discovery," Ben admitted with a shrug. "Found it by accident when I was trying to avoid some overzealous upperclassman who thought scholarship students didn't belong here."

Isabella leaned back against the wall, the weight of constant surveillance easing slightly for the first time in days. "I can't believe this place exists. Why didn't you show me sooner?"

"You didn't need it before," Ben said, his gaze steady. "Now you do."

She hesitated, then nodded. "Yeah. I guess I do."

They sat in silence for a moment, the muted sounds of the library filtering through the cracks in the shelves. The quiet felt different here—safe, almost sacred.

"I get why you're pushing back," Ben said finally, breaking the silence. "It's the only way to feel like you still have a say in your own life."

Isabella looked at him, surprised by the sudden vulnerability in his voice. "But?"

"But it's dangerous," he said, his expression serious. "You think ignoring Thorne is a victory, but he's not the kind of person who lets things go unnoticed. Sooner or later, he'll push back, and when he does, it won't be subtle."

"I know that," Isabella said, her voice firmer than she expected. "But I can't just keep letting him control me. I need this. Even if it's risky."

Ben studied her, his gaze lingering for a moment before he nodded. "Just promise me you'll be careful. This place... it takes people apart piece by piece if you let it."

"I'm not planning on letting it," Isabella said.

"Good," Ben said, leaning back with a faint smile. "Because I'd hate to lose my favorite sparring partner."

She rolled her eyes, though a small smile tugged at her lips. "Flattery doesn't suit you."

"Neither does worrying about other people," he countered. "And yet, here we are."

They both laughed softly, the sound muffled but genuine. For the first time in weeks, Isabella felt the knot of tension in her chest loosen slightly.

"This place is... nice," she said after a moment, her voice quieter now. "Thanks for showing it to me."

"Don't mention it," Ben replied. "Just don't tell anyone else. The fewer people know, the safer it stays."

"Agreed," Isabella said, glancing around the small space. It felt like a haven, a bubble of peace in a world that had grown increasingly suffocating.

As they sat there, the weight of the Syndicate's control seemed a little less crushing. For now, at least, she had found a place where she could breathe—and someone she could trust to share it with.

The quiet of Isabella's dorm room was punctuated only by the scratch of her pen against paper. She sat at her desk, Thorne's latest assignment spread out before her. The task seemed straightforward enough—an analysis of leadership dynamics in historical institutions—but something about it had been gnawing at her since she started.

The essay prompt was riddled with phrases that felt oddly specific, references that didn't align with the usual academic tone Thorne demanded. She flipped back through the pages, her eyes narrowing as she traced the lines of text.

"Carter," a familiar voice called softly from the open window.

Isabella turned sharply, startled to see Ben leaning casually against the sill. "Do you ever knock?" she hissed, her heart racing.

"Wouldn't be as fun," Ben replied, climbing inside. "What's got you so jumpy?"

"Nothing," she said quickly, though her gaze flicked back to the assignment in front of her.

Ben's eyes followed hers, and he raised an eyebrow. "Thorne's masterpiece?"

"Something like that," Isabella muttered, closing the folder as he approached.

Ben leaned against the desk, crossing his arms. "What's he got you doing this time?"

"Just another essay," she said, her voice nonchalant. "Leadership structures, historical influence, the usual."

"And yet you look like you've seen a ghost," Ben said, smirking.

"It's not the assignment," Isabella admitted, sighing. "It's... something else. These phrases he's using—they don't feel right."

Ben tilted his head, intrigued. "What kind of phrases?"

She hesitated, then pulled the folder open again, pointing to a line near the top of the first page. "'Leverage through alignment'—that's not exactly standard academic jargon, is it?"

Ben frowned, leaning closer to read. "Definitely not. Sounds more like something out of a corporate manifesto."

"Exactly," Isabella said, flipping to another page. "And look at this: 'Strategic compliance ensures longevity.' Who writes like that for a history essay?"

Ben's smirk faded, replaced by a more serious expression. "Thorne does, apparently. But why?"

"I don't know," Isabella said, her frustration clear. "But it feels like there's something else here, something he's not saying outright."

Ben was silent for a moment, his gaze fixed on the page. Then he straightened, his tone thoughtful. "Have you tried breaking it down? Could be code."

"Code?" Isabella repeated, raising an eyebrow.

"Yeah," Ben said. "Look at it—phrases like that don't just happen. Either he's messing with you, or there's something buried in the text."

She hesitated, then nodded slowly. "Okay, but how do I figure out if it's code?"

Ben grinned. "Lucky for you, I've got a talent for this sort of thing."

He pulled up a chair and began scanning the pages, muttering to himself as he worked. Isabella watched, a mix of curiosity and apprehension swirling in her chest.

"Here," Ben said after a few minutes, tapping a line near the bottom of one page. "'Alignment is rewarded; dissent is corrected.'"

"That's not exactly subtle," Isabella said, her unease deepening.

"No, but look at the structure," Ben said, pointing to the first letter of each word in the phrase. "A, I, R, D, I, C—what if the first letters spell something?"

Isabella leaned closer, her mind racing. "AIR… DIC?"

"Doesn't mean much on its own," Ben admitted. "But what if there are more phrases like this? Enough to form a message?"

They worked in silence for the next hour, pulling apart the text line by line. Slowly, a pattern emerged. Each page contained a phrase where the first letters of certain words spelled something out.

Finally, Isabella pieced together the fragmented letters. Her breath caught as the words took shape: **"Observe loyalty. Enforce compliance. Control remains absolute."**

"Control remains absolute," she repeated aloud, her voice barely above a whisper.

Ben sat back, his expression dark. "Looks like Thorne's not just assigning essays. He's sending a message."

"To who?" Isabella asked, her pulse pounding. "And why would he leave it where I could find it?"

Ben's eyes narrowed. "Maybe you weren't supposed to find it. Or maybe he wanted you to."

The thought sent a chill down Isabella's spine. She stared at the papers, the weight of the hidden message pressing down on her.

"This isn't just an assignment," she said finally. "It's a test."

"Or a trap," Ben added.

They exchanged a tense look, the implications settling over them like a dark cloud. Whatever Thorne's intentions were, one thing was clear: she was deeper in the Syndicate's web than she'd realized.

And there was no turning back now.

Isabella entered Thorne's office with measured steps, her pulse quickening as she crossed the threshold. Thorne was seated behind his desk, a stack of neatly arranged papers before him. He looked up, his expression calm but with an undercurrent of something sharper.

"Miss Carter," he said smoothly, gesturing toward the chair opposite him. "Please, sit."

She sat down, clasping her hands tightly in her lap to keep them from fidgeting.

"I trust you've been finding the assignments manageable," Thorne began, his tone polite but laced with something pointed.

"They've been challenging, but I'm keeping up," Isabella replied, her voice steady.

Thorne tilted his head slightly, his gaze narrowing. "That's good to hear. However, I've noticed some... discrepancies in your recent output. A certain lack of thoroughness."

Isabella stiffened. "I've been prioritizing my coursework, ensuring my academic performance remains strong."

"Admirable," Thorne said, leaning forward slightly. "But you must understand, Miss Carter, that the tasks I assign you are not extracurricular. They are integral to your growth here at Barrington—and to your alignment with the values we uphold."

She resisted the urge to look away, meeting his gaze squarely. "I understand, Professor. I just thought my academics were the priority."

"Your academics are one priority," Thorne corrected, his voice soft but firm. "Loyalty, however, is paramount. It is the foundation upon which everything else is built. Without it, no amount of academic achievement will matter."

Isabella's fingers tightened in her lap. "I didn't mean to give the impression that I'm not loyal."

"Actions, Miss Carter," Thorne said, his tone cooling. "They speak louder than intentions. When tasks are delayed or approached with less than full commitment, it raises questions. Questions about focus. About dedication."

"I'm fully committed," Isabella said quickly, her chest tightening.

"Are you?" Thorne asked, raising an eyebrow. "Because loyalty is not something that can be divided. It must be absolute. Undivided."

The words sent a chill down her spine. She struggled to keep her voice steady. "I'm doing my best to balance everything. I didn't realize the tasks were time-sensitive."

"Everything at Barrington is time-sensitive," Thorne said, standing and walking around to lean against the edge of his desk. "This institution thrives on precision and commitment. Those who hesitate, who falter, often find themselves left behind."

She swallowed hard, the subtle threat in his words cutting through the air like a blade. "I'll do better."

Thorne's expression softened slightly, though his eyes remained sharp. "I have no doubt you will. You're a bright young woman, Miss Carter. Your potential is extraordinary. But potential, as I'm sure you understand, is meaningless without execution."

"I understand," she said quietly, her hands tightening into fists.

"Good," Thorne said, his smile returning. "Then I expect your future efforts to reflect that understanding. This is not a place for half-measures."

"I'll make sure of it," Isabella replied, her voice firm despite the weight pressing down on her.

Thorne pushed off the desk and returned to his seat, his demeanor once again calm and composed. "That will be all for now. But do keep in mind, Miss Carter, that loyalty is not just about fulfilling tasks. It's about embodying a mindset—a commitment to the greater good of this institution."

She nodded, rising to her feet. "I won't let you down."

"I trust you won't," Thorne said, his voice a mix of reassurance and warning. "Because at Barrington, loyalty is not negotiable."

The words followed her as she left the office, the door clicking shut behind her. Each step away from Thorne's desk felt heavier, the weight of his expectations pressing down on her shoulders.

His reprimand had been subtle, but the message was clear: there was no room for error, no space for independence. The Syndicate's control was absolute, and any deviation from their expectations would come at a price.

Isabella clenched her fists, her resolve hardening. She wasn't sure how she would navigate the path ahead, but one thing was certain: she wouldn't let them break her.

Chapter 11
Shattered Alliances

The library's mezzanine was quieter than usual, its dimly lit corners offering a sense of seclusion. Isabella sat at their usual table, her books spread out but untouched as she checked her watch for the third time. Rachel was late, which was unlike her.

Frowning, Isabella pulled out her phone and typed a quick message: **You coming?**

The reply came almost instantly: **Not sure. I don't think I can tonight.**

Isabella stared at the screen, her frown deepening. She typed back: **What's going on? You never cancel.**

A long pause followed before the reply came: **Just not feeling it. Sorry.**

Determined, Isabella gathered her things and headed to Rachel's dorm. She knocked lightly, leaning closer to the door. "Rachel? It's me."

After a few moments, the door creaked open just wide enough to reveal Rachel's face. Her usually confident demeanor was absent, replaced by an anxious, almost skittish energy.

"Hey," Isabella said, her concern deepening. "What's wrong?"

"Nothing," Rachel said quickly, glancing over her shoulder as if expecting someone to appear. "I just... I'm not in the mood to study tonight."

"That's not like you," Isabella pressed, lowering her voice. "Did something happen?"

Rachel hesitated, her fingers tightening on the edge of the door. "I don't know what you're talking about."

"You're acting weird," Isabella said, stepping closer. "Come on, talk to me."

Rachel sighed, opening the door wider and motioning for Isabella to come inside. Once the door was shut, Rachel leaned against it, her arms crossed tightly over her chest.

"I just don't think it's a good idea to meet in the library anymore," Rachel said, her voice low.

"Why not?" Isabella asked, dropping her bag onto Rachel's bed.

Rachel hesitated, her gaze darting to the window. "It doesn't feel... safe. Not anymore."

"Safe?" Isabella repeated, her chest tightening. "What do you mean?"

Rachel shook her head, her jaw tightening. "You wouldn't understand."

"Try me," Isabella said, her voice firm.

Rachel hesitated again before finally speaking, her voice barely above a whisper. "I think... I think they're watching us."

"The Syndicate?" Isabella asked, her pulse quickening.

Rachel nodded, wrapping her arms around herself. "I don't know how, but I can feel it. Every time I go into the library, it's like there are eyes on me. I can't focus. I can't breathe."

"You've felt this before?" Isabella asked, stepping closer.

"Not like this," Rachel admitted, her voice trembling. "It's worse now. Like they're waiting for me to mess up."

Isabella's mind raced, her thoughts darting to the hidden cameras she'd already discovered. "Rachel, if they're watching you, it's because they think you know something. Do you?"

Rachel's head snapped up, her eyes wide. "No! I mean, I don't think so. I've kept my head down, just like you said. I haven't done anything wrong."

"Then why would they target you?" Isabella pressed.

"I don't know!" Rachel said, her voice breaking. She sank onto the edge of her bed, burying her face in her hands. "Maybe it's because I talk to you. Maybe it's because I've been too nosy. I don't know, okay?"

Isabella sat down beside her, placing a hand on her shoulder. "Hey, it's okay. We'll figure this out."

Rachel looked up at her, her expression filled with doubt. "You don't get it, Carter. You're strong. You don't let them scare you. But me? I'm not like that. I can't do this."

"You're doing better than you think," Isabella said softly. "You're still here, aren't you?"

"For now," Rachel muttered, her voice hollow.

The room fell into a tense silence, broken only by the faint hum of the radiator. Isabella's mind spun with possibilities, but one thought stood out above the rest: Rachel's fear wasn't baseless. The Syndicate's reach was everywhere, and if Rachel was feeling the pressure, it meant they were closing in.

"Look," Isabella said finally, her voice steady. "If they're watching you, we'll figure out why. And if they're trying to scare you, it's because they're afraid of what we might do. We're not powerless, Rachel."

Rachel shook her head, her eyes brimming with unshed tears. "That's easy for you to say. You don't know what it's like to feel like they could take everything from you in an instant."

Isabella's chest tightened, the weight of Rachel's words pressing down on her. "You're not alone in this," she said firmly. "Whatever happens, we'll face it together."

Rachel didn't respond, but the faintest glimmer of hope flickered in her expression. Isabella stood, determination hardening in her chest. The Syndicate's shadow loomed large, but she wouldn't let it crush them.

Not without a fight.

The quad was quiet, the late afternoon light casting long shadows across the cobblestones. Rachel and Isabella sat on a low stone wall near the edge of campus, their voices low as the wind rustled through the trees.

"I'm serious, Isabella," Rachel said, her tone sharper than usual. "You need to stop asking questions."

Isabella frowned, crossing her arms. "Why? Because they might hear me?"

"Yes," Rachel replied, her voice dropping to a near whisper. She glanced around, her eyes scanning for anyone nearby. "Because they're always listening."

"You don't know that," Isabella countered, though her voice lacked conviction.

Rachel turned to her, her expression grim. "Don't I? You've seen the cameras, the way they monitor everything we do. How many more signs do you need?"

"They can't control everything," Isabella said, trying to sound confident.

Rachel laughed bitterly. "That's what Ethan thought, too. And look where it got him."

The name sent a chill through Isabella. She leaned closer. "What happened to Ethan?"

Rachel hesitated, her fingers fidgeting with the hem of her jacket. "He was like you. Smart. Determined. Thought he could figure out the Syndicate's secrets."

"And?" Isabella pressed.

"And one day, he was gone," Rachel said bluntly. "No warning. No explanation. Just... gone. His dorm was emptied out by the end of the week, like he'd never even been here."

Isabella's breath caught. "Did anyone ask what happened?"

"Of course not," Rachel snapped. "Do you think anyone wanted to be next? Everyone just pretended he'd transferred or dropped out. But we all knew the truth."

"What truth?" Isabella demanded.

"That he dug too deep," Rachel said, her voice trembling. "He asked the wrong questions, trusted the wrong people. And the Syndicate made sure he wouldn't be a problem anymore."

Isabella stared at her, the weight of her words sinking in. "How do you know all this?"

"Because I saw it happen," Rachel admitted, her eyes glistening with unshed tears. "We were friends. Not close, but close enough. He told me things—things I shouldn't have known. And after he disappeared, I started getting notes."

"Notes?" Isabella asked, her heart pounding.

Rachel nodded, her voice dropping even lower. "Warnings. Nothing direct, just little reminders to 'stay focused' and 'mind my place.' I was terrified. I still am."

Isabella reached out, placing a hand on Rachel's arm. "Why didn't you tell me this before?"

"Because I thought you'd be smart enough to keep your head down," Rachel said, pulling away. "But you're not. You're just like Ethan, poking around, thinking you're invincible. You're not."

"I'm not trying to get myself expelled," Isabella said defensively. "I just... I need to understand what's going on."

"No, you don't," Rachel said firmly. "You need to survive. And the only way to do that is to stop asking questions and do what they tell you."

"Rachel," Isabella began, but her friend cut her off.

"No," Rachel said, her voice shaking. "You think you're so clever, but you have no idea what they're capable of. If you keep this up, they'll come for you, just like they came for Ethan."

Isabella fell silent, the weight of Rachel's fear pressing down on her. "I'm not going to let them scare me into submission," she said finally, her voice quiet but resolute.

Rachel shook her head, tears spilling down her cheeks. "Then you're a fool. And I don't want to watch you disappear, too."

The words cut deep, but Isabella refused to back down. "I'm not going anywhere," she said, her tone firm. "I promise."

"You can't promise that," Rachel whispered, her voice breaking. "Not here. Not with them watching."

As the silence stretched between them, Isabella realized just how high the stakes were. Rachel's warning was more than fear—it was a desperate plea. But for Isabella, it only fueled her determination.

The Syndicate's shadow loomed large, but she wasn't ready to back down. Not yet.

The dorm room felt stifling, the air heavy with unspoken tension. Isabella stood near the window, arms crossed, her gaze locked on Rachel. Across the room, Rachel sat on the edge of her bed, her hands gripping the sides as if the pressure might anchor her.

"You've been holding back," Isabella said, her tone sharper than she intended. "And I need to know why."

Rachel flinched but didn't look up. "I don't know what you're talking about."

"Don't," Isabella said, stepping closer. "Don't lie to me. I can't afford it—not now."

"I'm not lying," Rachel muttered, her voice trembling.

"You've hinted at things, dropped warnings, but you've never told me the whole truth," Isabella pressed. "Why? What are you so afraid of?"

Rachel's head snapped up, her eyes glistening with unshed tears. "Everything, Isabella! I'm afraid of everything. Isn't that enough for you?"

Isabella hesitated, the raw emotion in Rachel's voice catching her off guard. "No, it's not. I need to understand what we're up against. You've seen more than you're letting on, and if I don't know the truth, how am I supposed to fight this?"

"Fight?" Rachel let out a bitter laugh. "You can't fight them, Carter. That's what you don't get. That's what you'll never get."

"Then help me understand!" Isabella said, her voice rising. "If you know something, anything, that could make sense of this, I need you to tell me."

Rachel's hands clenched into fists, her whole body shaking. "You think I know what's going on? You think I have some secret key to unraveling the Syndicate? I don't, Isabella! I don't know anything—because they don't let us know anything!"

"Rachel—" Isabella began, but Rachel cut her off, her voice cracking.

"No! You don't get it. You keep pushing, and you think you're so clever, but all you're doing is making yourself a target. And me? I'm already a target just for knowing you!"

Isabella felt her chest tighten. "I never asked you to put yourself at risk."

"You didn't have to," Rachel said bitterly. "The moment you started asking questions, they started watching you. And anyone close to you? They get caught in the crossfire."

The words hit like a slap, but Isabella didn't back down. "That doesn't explain why you've been so vague. You know more than you're letting on, Rachel. You're hiding something."

Tears spilled down Rachel's cheeks, and she shook her head. "You think I'm hiding something? Fine. You're right. I am."

"Then tell me," Isabella said, her voice softening.

Rachel looked up, her eyes red-rimmed and brimming with despair. "You want to know the truth? The truth is, I don't know who I can trust anymore. Not you. Not anyone. Every word I say feels like it's being recorded, every move I make like it's being judged. I've tried to stay out of it, to stay safe, but it doesn't matter. They've already decided who I am."

"Rachel," Isabella said quietly, taking a step closer.

"They make you feel like a pawn," Rachel continued, her voice breaking. "Like no matter what you do, they've already planned out the whole game. And maybe they have. Maybe there's no way out of this."

"There is a way," Isabella said firmly, kneeling in front of her. "We just have to find it. Together."

Rachel let out a shaky breath, her hands covering her face. "You don't get it, Isabella. They're not just watching us. They're controlling us. They decide who succeeds, who fails, who disappears. And if you step out of line, they'll crush you without a second thought."

"Then why haven't they crushed me yet?" Isabella asked, her voice steady.

Rachel looked at her, her expression filled with a mix of fear and frustration. "Because they're waiting. Watching. Testing you. And if you keep pushing, they won't wait much longer."

The silence that followed was heavy, the weight of Rachel's words settling over them like a storm cloud. Isabella reached out, placing a hand on Rachel's shoulder.

"I'm not going to let them win," she said softly. "Not without a fight."

Rachel shook her head, her tears falling freely now. "You don't understand. There's no winning against them. There's only surviving. And I don't know if I can do even that anymore."

Isabella squeezed her shoulder, her own resolve hardening. "Then I'll fight for both of us."

Rachel let out a shaky laugh, though it was tinged with bitterness. "You're stubborn, you know that?"

"I've been told," Isabella replied, a faint smile breaking through her worry.

The room fell quiet again, the tension still thick but less oppressive. Rachel wiped her face with the sleeve of her jacket, her breathing gradually evening out.

For the first time, Isabella saw just how deeply the Syndicate's grip had sunk into Rachel's life. She wasn't just scared—she was broken. And that made Isabella's determination burn even brighter.

The Syndicate had taken so much from them already. She wasn't going to let them take any more.

The rain outside Rachel's dorm room window tapped against the glass like an unrelenting reminder of the storm brewing inside. Rachel sat cross-legged on her bed, her shoulders hunched as if trying to shrink into herself. Isabella paced the small room, her movements sharp and deliberate.

"You can't keep living like this, Rachel," Isabella said, her voice tight with frustration. "Afraid of every shadow, second-guessing every word."

Rachel glanced up, her eyes rimmed with exhaustion. "Do you think I want to? You think I like feeling like this?"

"No, but they do," Isabella said, stopping in her tracks to face Rachel. "This is what they want—to keep you scared and compliant. To make you believe there's no way out."

Rachel scoffed, shaking her head. "Because there isn't. Not for me, not for you, not for anyone. You can't win against them, Isabella. They're too powerful."

"Maybe they are," Isabella admitted, her voice softening. "But that doesn't mean we stop trying."

Rachel let out a bitter laugh, her fingers gripping the edge of her blanket. "You sound like Ethan."

"Good," Isabella shot back. "Because he was right to ask questions. And you know it."

Rachel's expression faltered, and she looked away, her voice trembling. "Look where it got him."

"That's not going to happen to you," Isabella said firmly, sitting down on the edge of the bed. "I won't let it."

Rachel looked at her, her eyes filled with a mix of fear and disbelief. "You can't promise that. You don't even know what you're up against."

"You're right—I don't," Isabella said, her tone steady. "But I do know this: as long as they keep us scared and divided, they win. And I'm not going to let them win."

Rachel shook her head again, her voice breaking. "You don't understand. They don't just punish you for asking questions—they erase you. They make you disappear, like you never existed. How are we supposed to fight that?"

"By sticking together," Isabella said, placing a hand on Rachel's arm. "By refusing to let them isolate us. They're not invincible, Rachel. They want us to think they are, but they're not."

Rachel pulled her knees to her chest, her voice barely above a whisper. "I don't know if I can do this."

"You don't have to," Isabella said gently. "Not alone."

Rachel's gaze met hers, the vulnerability in her eyes striking a chord deep within Isabella. In that moment, she realized just how much Rachel had been carrying on her own, how deeply the Syndicate's shadow had taken hold of her.

"I'll protect you," Isabella said quietly but with conviction. "Whatever it takes, I'll make sure they don't hurt you."

Rachel's lip quivered, and for a moment, it looked like she might cry again. "Why would you do that? You don't owe me anything."

"Because you're my friend," Isabella replied simply. "And because someone has to stand up to them."

Rachel let out a shaky breath, wiping her eyes with the back of her hand. "You're going to get yourself killed, you know that?"

"Maybe," Isabella said with a faint smile. "But at least I'll go down fighting."

Rachel laughed weakly, the sound bittersweet. "You're impossible."

"And you're stuck with me," Isabella replied, squeezing Rachel's arm before standing.

The rain outside had slowed to a drizzle, the room falling into a hushed silence. Isabella stood by the window, her gaze distant as she watched the droplets streak down the glass.

Her doubts about the Syndicate were no longer just whispers at the back of her mind—they were a storm, building stronger with each passing day. She didn't have all the answers, and the stakes felt higher than ever.

But as she looked back at Rachel, who was slowly beginning to breathe easier, Isabella knew one thing for certain: she couldn't walk away.

The Syndicate thrived on fear and silence. It was time to break both.

And if that meant stepping into the line of fire, so be it.

Chapter 12
Family Ties and False Truths

The dining hall was unusually quiet for a Friday evening. Isabella sat across from Adam at a corner table, her untouched coffee growing cold in its cup. Adam leaned back in his chair, his usual charm subdued, a rare stillness settling over him as he stared out the window.

"You've been quiet lately," Isabella said, breaking the silence.

Adam glanced at her, a faint smile tugging at his lips. "Have I?"

"Not exactly your style," Isabella replied, raising an eyebrow. "Usually, you're all confidence and witty one-liners. What's going on?"

Adam shrugged, his gaze drifting back to the view outside. "Guess I'm not in the mood to perform tonight."

"Perform?" Isabella asked, leaning forward slightly. "Is that what it feels like to you?"

"Sometimes," Adam admitted, his tone soft but carrying a weight she hadn't heard before. "Everyone expects me to be a certain way—always polished, always perfect. It gets exhausting."

Isabella studied him, her curiosity growing. "Who's everyone?"

Adam hesitated, his fingers tapping absently against the table. "My parents, mostly. Their friends. The board members at Barrington. Anyone who's invested in the 'Sinclair legacy.'"

"The Sinclair legacy?" Isabella repeated, frowning.

Adam let out a bitter laugh, his smile fading. "You've heard of Sinclair Industries, right? One of the biggest corporate empires in the country? That's my family. And they've made it very clear that I'm expected to uphold the brand."

"Sounds... intense," Isabella said carefully.

"You have no idea," Adam replied, running a hand through his hair. "Every move I make, every grade I earn, every relationship I have—it's all scrutinized. Everything I do has to reflect well on the family. No mistakes allowed."

Isabella tilted her head, her mind racing. "Is that why the Syndicate's so interested in you? Because of your family?"

Adam stiffened slightly, his eyes narrowing. "What do you know about the Syndicate?"

"Not much," Isabella admitted. "Just enough to know they're watching everyone—and that they seem especially invested in you."

Adam let out a slow breath, his shoulders slumping. "Yeah, well, they've made it pretty clear that they see me as an asset. Or maybe a liability, depending on the day."

"Why?" Isabella asked, leaning closer.

Adam hesitated, his jaw tightening. "Because they know about the cracks. The scandals my parents have spent years trying to cover up. The things they'll do anything to keep buried."

"What kind of scandals?" Isabella pressed gently.

Adam's lips pressed into a thin line, and he shook his head. "It doesn't matter. What matters is that the Syndicate knows—and they're using it to keep me in line."

Isabella's stomach churned at the bitterness in his voice. "That's not right."

Adam let out a humorless laugh. "Since when has right mattered at Barrington? The Syndicate doesn't care about morality. They care about power, control, and leverage. And they've got plenty of it when it comes to me."

"Have they threatened you?" Isabella asked, her voice dropping to a near whisper.

"Not directly," Adam said, his gaze fixed on the table. "But they don't have to. The implications are always there. Do as they say, keep the family's image clean, and they'll leave me alone. Step out of line, and... well, you can guess the rest."

Isabella frowned, her thoughts swirling. She'd always known the Syndicate was dangerous, but hearing Adam's story made their methods feel even more insidious.

"Why are you telling me this?" she asked finally.

Adam's eyes met hers, a flicker of vulnerability breaking through his usual composure. "Because I'm tired, Isabella. Tired of pretending everything's fine when it's not. And because... I think you might actually understand."

She swallowed hard, her resolve hardening. "You don't have to go through this alone."

Adam smiled faintly, though it didn't reach his eyes. "Thanks, but I've been dealing with this my whole life. I don't think I know how to do it any other way."

"Well, maybe it's time to learn," Isabella said firmly.

The silence that followed was heavy but not uncomfortable. Isabella studied Adam, the cracks in his confident exterior revealing someone far more complex—and far more vulnerable—than she'd expected.

For the first time, she saw Adam not as an untouchable golden boy but as someone who, like her, was trapped in the Syndicate's web. And for the first time, she felt a flicker of determination to help him find a way out.

The library was eerily quiet, the usual murmur of students replaced by the hum of fluorescent lights and the occasional creak of floorboards. Isabella sat at a desk in the far corner, her laptop open and a series of files spread out before her. The digital archive's interface was clunky, but it held an extensive repository of Barrington's history and financial records.

"Come on," Isabella muttered under her breath, scrolling through yet another page of unremarkable entries. She had been digging for hours, searching for anything that might explain why the Syndicate was so interested in Adam Sinclair.

Finally, her eyes landed on something unusual: **Sinclair Industries: Partnered Initiatives with Barrington Alumni Trust.**

Her heart quickened as she clicked the link. A list of projects appeared, each accompanied by dates and funding sources. At first glance, it seemed innocuous—corporate sponsorships for research, scholarships, and campus renovations. But as she dug deeper, patterns began to emerge.

"Found something?"

Isabella jumped, her hand flying to her chest. She looked up to see Ben leaning casually against a nearby bookshelf, his usual smirk firmly in place.

"Do you have to sneak up on people like that?" she hissed.

"Only when they look like they're hiding something," Ben replied, pulling out a chair and sitting beside her. "What are you working on?"

She hesitated, her eyes darting back to the screen. "Just research."

Ben raised an eyebrow. "Research on what?"

"Adam," Isabella admitted reluctantly.

Ben leaned closer, his interest clearly piqued. "And?"

She gestured to the screen. "And I think I just found something big. Look at this."

Ben's eyes scanned the list, his brow furrowing. "Sinclair Industries? That's his family's company, right?"

"Right," Isabella said, clicking on one of the entries. "And look at this—'Project Alignment: Funded by Sinclair Industries in collaboration with Barrington Alumni Trust.'"

"Alignment?" Ben repeated, his tone skeptical. "That doesn't sound shady at all."

"Exactly," Isabella said. "And it's not the only one. There's a whole list of projects here—each one tied to Sinclair Industries and each one partially funded by Syndicate-associated groups."

Ben frowned, leaning back in his chair. "So, what does it mean?"

"I don't know yet," Isabella admitted. "But it can't be a coincidence. The Syndicate isn't just interested in Adam because of who he is—they're interested in his family. They've been working together for years."

Ben let out a low whistle, his expression darkening. "That's a pretty big connection to hide in plain sight."

Isabella nodded, her fingers flying over the keyboard as she opened another document. "There has to be more. Something that explains why they're so invested in him."

"Or why they're so interested in keeping him in line," Ben added.

They worked in silence for a few minutes, the weight of their discovery settling over them like a heavy fog. Isabella's mind raced as she pieced together the implications. The Syndicate wasn't just a shadowy group pulling strings behind the scenes—they were deeply embedded in Barrington's operations, and Adam's family was at the heart of it.

"This changes everything," Isabella said finally, her voice barely above a whisper.

"Does it?" Ben asked, his tone cautious. "We already knew the Syndicate had their claws in this place. Now we just know how deep they go."

"It's not just Barrington," Isabella said, turning to face him. "It's bigger than that. If Sinclair Industries is involved, who knows how far their influence reaches?"

Ben's jaw tightened, his usual smirk replaced by a rare seriousness. "And what are you planning to do with all this information?"

"I don't know yet," Isabella admitted. "But I can't just ignore it."

"You need to be careful," Ben said, his voice low. "If the Syndicate finds out you're digging into this, they won't just sit back and let you keep going."

"I know," Isabella said, her resolve hardening. "But if we don't figure this out, who will?"

Ben didn't respond immediately, his gaze fixed on the screen. Finally, he sighed, leaning back in his chair. "You've got guts, Carter. I'll give you that."

"Thanks," she said, offering a faint smile.

"But guts won't save you if you get caught," he added.

"I'll take my chances," Isabella replied, turning back to her laptop.

The tension between them was thick, but Ben didn't press further. Isabella's mind was already miles ahead, trying to unravel the threads of the Syndicate's web.

As she closed the files and logged out of the archive, one thought lingered: Adam wasn't just a pawn in the Syndicate's game—he was a piece of the puzzle.

And now, so was she.

The quiet of the campus garden was a rare reprieve from the constant hum of Barrington's controlled chaos. Isabella sat on a stone bench, her gaze on the fountain at the center of the garden. Adam stood a few feet away, his hands shoved deep into the pockets of his coat as he paced slowly along the gravel path.

"I never asked for any of this," Adam said suddenly, his voice breaking the silence.

Isabella turned to look at him, surprised by the bitterness in his tone. "Any of what?"

"This," he said, gesturing vaguely at the campus around them. "Barrington, the Syndicate, all the expectations. It's like... I'm playing a role in someone else's script, and I don't even know the ending."

"You seem to handle it well enough," Isabella replied carefully.

"That's because I don't have a choice," Adam said, stopping in front of her. "Do you know what it's like to have your entire life mapped out for you before you even understand what it means to be alive? To be told who you are, who you'll become, and what's expected of you—without ever being asked what you want?"

She shook her head, her chest tightening at the raw emotion in his voice. "No, I don't. But I can imagine it's suffocating."

"It is," Adam said, his jaw tightening. He sat down beside her, running a hand through his hair. "And Barrington is just another link in the chain. They don't care about us as people—they care about what we represent. Assets, liabilities, potential threats."

"What do you mean by threats?" Isabella asked, her curiosity piqued.

Adam hesitated, his gaze fixed on the fountain. "The Syndicate. They don't just reward loyalty—they demand it. And if you don't fall in line, they make your life hell. Or worse."

"Has that happened to you?" Isabella asked, her voice soft.

Adam didn't answer right away, his shoulders slumping as he exhaled slowly. "Not yet. But I see the signs. The way they keep tabs on me, the subtle reminders that they know everything about my family, my history. It's their way of making sure I don't forget who's really in charge."

"Why do you stay?" Isabella asked, leaning closer.

"Because I don't have a choice," Adam said, his voice low. "Leaving isn't an option. Not for someone like me. If I walk away, I lose everything—my family's support, my future, my name. And even if I did leave, the Syndicate would make sure I couldn't go far."

Isabella's stomach churned at the despair in his words. "That's not right, Adam. You shouldn't have to live like that."

He let out a humorless laugh. "Welcome to Barrington, where nothing is right and everything is a transaction."

They sat in silence for a moment, the only sound the faint trickle of water from the fountain. Isabella's mind raced, torn between her growing sympathy for Adam and the weight of her own secret. Her task—to observe him, to report back to Thorne—felt more unethical with every passing second.

"You're different, you know," Adam said suddenly, breaking her thoughts.

"What do you mean?" she asked, startled.

"You don't play their game," Adam said, his gaze meeting hers. "You don't pretend to be something you're not. It's... refreshing."

Isabella's chest tightened, guilt creeping in. "Maybe I'm just good at hiding it," she said softly.

Adam smiled faintly. "Maybe. But I think there's more to you than that."

The sincerity in his voice caught her off guard, and for a moment, she couldn't find the words to respond. Instead, she looked away, her thoughts swirling.

"I don't know how much longer I can do this," Adam admitted, his voice barely above a whisper. "But I'm not sure I have the strength to stop."

"You do," Isabella said firmly, turning back to him. "You're stronger than you think, Adam. And you're not alone in this."

He looked at her, a flicker of hope breaking through the darkness in his eyes. "You mean that?"

"Yes," she said, her voice steady. "I mean it."

The silence that followed felt heavy but not uncomfortable. Isabella's resolve solidified as she sat beside Adam, their shared understanding deepening the bond between them.

But even as she made her silent promise to help him, the weight of her own role pressed down on her. She wasn't just a confidant—she was a spy. And the longer she stayed close to Adam, the harder it would be to reconcile the two.

For now, she pushed the guilt aside. Adam needed someone to believe in him, and for as long as she could, Isabella would be that person.

Even if it meant walking an increasingly dangerous line.

Thorne's office felt colder than usual, the dim light from the desk lamp casting long shadows across the polished wood. Isabella sat across from him, her hands folded tightly in her lap, her heart pounding as he reviewed the report she had hastily written the night before.

"This is... vague," Thorne said finally, setting the paper down and folding his hands on the desk.

Isabella forced herself to meet his gaze. "I reported everything I observed."

"Did you?" Thorne asked, his voice calm but laced with skepticism. "Because I find it hard to believe that someone like Adam Sinclair is as unremarkable as this report suggests."

She swallowed hard, her pulse quickening. "He keeps to himself most of the time. Studies, attends meetings, goes to class. There's not much to report."

Thorne leaned back in his chair, studying her with a piercing gaze. "Miss Carter, you're intelligent enough to know that I'm not looking for routine details. The Syndicate doesn't waste resources on 'unremarkable.' We need insight. Patterns. Vulnerabilities."

"I'm doing my best," Isabella said, her voice steady despite the turmoil churning inside her.

"Are you?" Thorne pressed, leaning forward slightly. "Because what I see here is the bare minimum. And I know you're capable of much more."

She hesitated, her thoughts racing. "Adam is careful," she said finally. "He doesn't let people in easily. If I push too hard, he'll notice."

Thorne tilted his head, a faint smile playing at his lips. "A fair point. But you'll need to find a way around that. The Syndicate doesn't accept obstacles, Miss Carter. We overcome them."

"What exactly are you looking for?" she asked, stalling for time.

"Anything that can help us understand him better," Thorne replied. "His motivations, his weaknesses, his loyalties. Adam Sinclair is a valuable asset, but assets must be managed carefully. And to manage him, we need information."

Isabella nodded slowly, her chest tightening. "I understand."

"I hope so," Thorne said, his tone softening slightly. "Because loyalty is not just about action—it's about intent. Half-measures suggest doubt, and doubt is... unhelpful."

The unspoken warning hung in the air, and Isabella forced herself to stay composed. "I'll dig deeper," she said finally.

Thorne smiled faintly, though it didn't reach his eyes. "Good. I knew I could count on you."

She stood, eager to escape the oppressive weight of his gaze. But as she turned to leave, his voice stopped her.

"Miss Carter."

She froze, her hand on the door handle. "Yes, Professor?"

Thorne's smile lingered, his gaze sharp. "I expect progress by the end of the week. Don't disappoint me."

"I won't," Isabella said, her voice steady despite the knot in her stomach.

The walk back to her dorm was a blur, her mind spinning with the implications of what had just transpired. Thorne's demands were clear, and the stakes had never felt higher.

Sitting at her desk, she stared at her notebook, the empty page mocking her. The idea of betraying Adam, of feeding the Syndicate the details they craved, made her chest tighten with guilt. She couldn't do it—not after everything Adam had confided in her.

With a deep breath, she began to write, crafting another carefully worded report that revealed nothing of significance. It was a dangerous game, and she knew it wouldn't hold Thorne off forever.

As she finished, her hands trembled, the weight of her deception pressing down on her. Lying to Thorne had been easy in the moment, but the consequences loomed large.

For now, she had protected Adam. But at what cost?

Chapter 13
Loyalty on Trial

The study alcove was dimly lit, the soft glow of the old lamp casting long shadows across the stacks of books scattered on the table. Isabella sat with her head bowed, her notebook open but untouched. Her thoughts churned, Thorne's words echoing in her mind.

"You're playing a dangerous game, Carter."

The voice startled her, and she looked up to see Ben standing in the doorway, his arms crossed and his expression dark.

"What are you talking about?" Isabella asked, her voice steady but cautious.

Ben stepped inside, letting the door click shut behind him. "I saw you leaving Thorne's office. Again."

"So?" Isabella said, sitting up straighter.

"So," Ben said, his tone sharper now, "how many times are you going to march in there and let him pull your strings before you realize what you're doing?"

"I'm not letting him pull my strings," Isabella snapped.

"Aren't you?" Ben shot back, his eyes narrowing. "Because from where I'm standing, it looks like you're doing exactly what he wants."

Isabella stood, her fists clenching at her sides. "You don't know what you're talking about."

"Don't I?" Ben said, stepping closer. "You think I don't see what's happening? The way he's got you running around, spying on Adam, writing reports? You're playing right into their hands."

"I'm trying to survive," Isabella said, her voice rising. "Do you think I have a choice?"

"We always have a choice," Ben said coldly. "You're just too scared to make the right one."

"Don't you dare judge me," Isabella said, her voice shaking with anger. "You have no idea what it's like to be in my position."

Ben let out a bitter laugh. "No idea? Carter, I've been in your position. I've done exactly what you're doing, and I know how it ends. You think you're protecting yourself, but all you're doing is digging yourself deeper."

"Then what am I supposed to do?" Isabella demanded. "Walk away? Pretend they're not watching my every move? They'd crush me, Ben."

"They're already crushing you," Ben said, his voice softening slightly. "You're just too focused on surviving to notice."

Isabella looked away, her chest tightening. "It's not that simple."

"It is," Ben said, stepping closer. "The more you give them, the more power they have over you. You have to stop playing their game."

"And do what?" Isabella asked, her voice breaking. "Fight back? They'd destroy me, Ben. They'd destroy all of us."

"Maybe," Ben said quietly. "But at least you'd still have a piece of yourself left. Right now, you're letting them take that, too."

Isabella turned away, her hands trembling as she gripped the edge of the table. "I didn't ask for this," she said, her voice barely above a whisper.

"I know," Ben said, his tone softening further. "But you have to decide who you want to be. Because if you keep going down this path, you won't recognize yourself when it's over."

The room fell silent, the weight of his words hanging heavy in the air. Isabella closed her eyes, her mind spinning with doubt and fear.

"I'm scared, Ben," she admitted finally, her voice trembling. "I don't know how to fight them."

"Neither do I," Ben said, his voice steady but filled with frustration. "But we can figure it out together. You don't have to do this alone."

She turned to look at him, her eyes filled with uncertainty. "You really think we have a chance?"

"I don't know," Ben admitted, a faint smile tugging at his lips. "But I'd rather go down fighting than let them win without a fight."

Isabella let out a shaky breath, her anger ebbing away. "I don't know if I can do it."

"You can," Ben said firmly. "But you have to start by saying no to Thorne. No more reports. No more spying. No more letting them turn you into one of their pawns."

She nodded slowly, her resolve hardening. "Okay. No more."

Ben studied her for a moment, then nodded as well. "Good. Because if we're going to take them on, we need to be on the same side."

"We are," Isabella said, her voice steadier now.

The tension between them eased, though the enormity of what lay ahead loomed large. Isabella knew Ben was right—she had to stop playing the Syndicate's game.

But as she sat back down and stared at the notebook in front of her, she couldn't help but wonder if it was already too late.

The evening sky outside the dorm window was a wash of muted grays, matching the tension that filled Rachel's room. Rachel paced in tight circles near her desk, her fingers twisting the hem of her sweater. Isabella sat on the edge of the bed, watching her friend with a mix of concern and frustration.

"You're not listening to me," Rachel said, her voice rising slightly. "I'm telling you, this is too dangerous."

"I hear you, Rachel," Isabella replied evenly. "But doing nothing is dangerous too."

Rachel spun around, her eyes wide and brimming with fear. "No, it's not the same. Keeping your head down is survival. Poking at the Syndicate is suicide."

"Is it?" Isabella asked, crossing her arms. "Because last I checked, they don't need a reason to come after us. If they want to ruin our lives, they will, whether we stay silent or not."

Rachel shook her head, her voice trembling. "That's exactly why you need to stop. Don't give them a reason. Don't make yourself a target."

"I'm already a target," Isabella said, her tone sharpening. "We all are. But the difference is, I'm not willing to let them scare me into silence."

Rachel's pacing stopped abruptly, and she turned to face Isabella, her expression a mixture of frustration and desperation. "You think you're being brave, but you're not. You're being reckless. And you're going to drag me down with you."

Isabella stood, her chest tightening. "That's not fair, and you know it. I'm not asking you to do anything. I'm not even asking you to agree with me. But I can't just sit back and pretend like this is normal."

"Normal doesn't matter," Rachel snapped, her voice breaking. "What matters is staying safe. What matters is keeping our heads down and making it through this place alive."

"Alive, but at what cost?" Isabella asked, her voice softening. "Rachel, they've already taken so much from us. Our privacy, our choices, our sense of security. Are we just supposed to let them keep taking until there's nothing left?"

Rachel's shoulders slumped, and she sank into the chair by her desk, burying her face in her hands. "You don't understand, Isabella. You don't know what they're capable of."

"Then tell me," Isabella said, stepping closer. "Help me understand."

Rachel looked up, tears streaking her face. "Do you remember Ethan? The guy I told you about who disappeared?"

Isabella nodded, her heart sinking.

"I never told you the whole story," Rachel admitted, her voice barely above a whisper. "He wasn't just asking questions. He was trying to expose them. He thought he could outsmart them, and for a while, it seemed like he was winning. But then..." She trailed off, her voice cracking.

"But then what?" Isabella pressed gently.

Rachel took a shaky breath. "One day, he was just gone. No warning, no explanation. And the next week, everyone was pretending like he'd never even been here. The administration, the professors, even his so-called friends. It was like the Syndicate erased him from existence."

Isabella's stomach churned, but she forced herself to stay calm. "That doesn't mean they'll do the same to me."

"Doesn't it?" Rachel asked, her voice rising again. "You think you're special? You think they won't notice what you're doing? They're already watching you, Isabella. If you keep pushing, you're going to end up just like him."

"Maybe," Isabella said, her voice steady despite the fear clawing at her chest. "But maybe not. Maybe this time will be different."

Rachel let out a bitter laugh, shaking her head. "You're delusional."

"Maybe I am," Isabella admitted. "But I can't live like this, Rachel. I can't keep pretending everything's fine when it's not. If that makes me reckless, so be it. But I have to try."

Rachel stared at her, her expression a mixture of disbelief and sorrow. "You're going to get yourself killed, and for what? Some half-baked idea of justice?"

"For the chance to take back some control," Isabella said quietly. "For the chance to make things better, even if it's just a little."

The room fell into an uneasy silence, the weight of their argument settling heavily over them. Rachel turned away, her voice trembling as she spoke.

"Just promise me one thing," she said without looking at Isabella.

"What?"

"Be careful," Rachel whispered. "Because if they come for you, I won't be able to help you."

Isabella nodded, her chest tightening. "I will."

But even as she said the words, she knew the path ahead would only grow more dangerous. Rachel's fear was a constant reminder of the stakes, but it wasn't enough to deter her.

The Syndicate's grip was tightening, and Isabella couldn't stand by and do nothing. Not anymore.

The late afternoon sun filtered through the tall windows of the library, casting long shadows across the rows of bookshelves. Isabella sat at their usual table, her notebook open in front of her, but her mind far from the blank page. Across from her,

Adam leaned back in his chair, his arms crossed and his piercing gaze fixed on her.

"You've been... distracted lately," Adam said, breaking the silence.

Isabella glanced up, her heart skipping a beat at the intensity in his voice. "I've had a lot on my mind," she said carefully, trying to keep her tone light.

Adam tilted his head slightly, his expression unreadable. "A lot on your mind, or something you're not telling me?"

She stiffened, forcing herself to maintain eye contact. "What's that supposed to mean?"

"You tell me," Adam replied, leaning forward. "We've spent a lot of time together recently, but it feels like you're holding something back."

Isabella hesitated, her thoughts racing. "I'm not holding anything back," she said, though the words felt hollow even as she spoke them.

Adam raised an eyebrow, his gaze narrowing. "Really? Because it feels like every time I ask you something personal, you find a way to change the subject. And when I'm the one talking, it's like you're... taking notes."

Her stomach dropped, and she scrambled for a response. "That's not fair," she said, her voice a little too sharp. "I'm just trying to get to know you."

"Are you?" Adam asked, his tone cutting. "Because it feels like there's more to it than that."

Isabella looked away, her fingers tightening around her pen. "You're being paranoid."

"Am I?" Adam pressed. "Or is there something you don't want me to know?"

The tension between them thickened, the air heavy with unspoken accusations. Isabella's mind raced, guilt clawing at her chest. She had known this moment would come eventually, but she hadn't expected it to happen so soon—or so directly.

"Why would I hide something from you?" she asked, forcing herself to meet his gaze.

"That's what I'm trying to figure out," Adam said, his voice quieter now but no less intense. "You say you're my friend, but sometimes it feels like you're... watching me."

"I'm not watching you," Isabella said quickly, her voice trembling slightly. "I care about you, Adam. I wouldn't do that to you."

"Then prove it," Adam said, his eyes locked on hers. "Tell me the truth. What's going on?"

She opened her mouth, but the words wouldn't come. How could she tell him the truth without risking everything? Without destroying whatever trust they had left?

"I... I can't," she said finally, her voice barely above a whisper.

Adam's expression darkened, and he leaned back in his chair. "That's what I thought."

"It's not what you think," Isabella said, her desperation creeping into her voice.

"Then explain it to me," Adam said, his tone cold. "Because right now, it feels like I'm just a project to you. Something to study, to report on."

The accusation hit her like a blow, and she flinched. "You're not a project," she said, her voice trembling. "You're my friend."

"Then why does it feel like you're lying to me?" Adam asked, his voice rising slightly. "Why does it feel like I can't trust you?"

Isabella's chest tightened, the weight of her guilt threatening to crush her. "I'm trying to protect you," she said finally, her voice cracking.

Adam frowned, confusion flickering across his face. "Protect me? From what?"

She shook her head, unable to meet his gaze. "I can't explain. Not yet."

Adam let out a bitter laugh, pushing his chair back as he stood. "Not yet. Right. Because that makes this all so much better."

"Adam, please," Isabella said, standing as well. "You have to trust me."

"Why should I?" Adam asked, his voice cold. "You don't trust me enough to tell me the truth."

The words hung between them, cutting deeper than she'd expected. Adam turned and walked away, leaving her standing alone by the table, her hands trembling.

As the library's silence closed in around her, Isabella sank back into her chair, her head in her hands. Adam's growing distrust was understandable, even justified, but it didn't make it hurt any less.

She had chosen this path, knowing it would lead to moments like this. But the reality of losing his trust—and the risk of losing him entirely—was harder to bear than she had imagined.

For the first time, she wondered if her mission was worth the cost.

The campus courtyard was bathed in moonlight, casting elongated shadows across the cobblestones. Isabella paced in slow, deliberate steps, her mind racing. The day's events replayed over and over—the argument with Ben, Rachel's desperate warnings, Adam's piercing accusations. They were all warning her to stop, to abandon her plans before it was too late. But she couldn't shake the nagging thought: If not her, then who?

She stopped at the edge of the fountain, staring into the rippling water. Her reflection stared back, fractured and distorted. It felt fitting. Every decision she'd made since coming to Barrington seemed to pull her further away from who she thought she was. Yet, even now, as guilt gnawed at her, she couldn't bring herself to stop.

Her phone vibrated in her pocket. She pulled it out and saw a message from Rachel: **"Please, don't do anything stupid."**

Isabella sighed, slipping the phone back into her pocket without replying. She couldn't make Rachel understand. This wasn't about recklessness—it was about necessity. If she stayed silent, if she kept playing along, she'd lose herself entirely.

Later that night, in the dim light of the library, Isabella sifted through the papers she'd carefully hidden over the past few weeks. Assignment notes, reports she'd written for Thorne, fragments of information she'd overheard in passing—all of it was spread out before her like pieces of a puzzle. Somewhere in these pages, she hoped, was the key to exposing the Syndicate.

The creak of a chair startled her. She looked up to see Ben sitting across from her, his expression unreadable.

"You're at it again," he said, his voice low.

Isabella didn't respond, her eyes flicking back to the papers.

Ben leaned forward, resting his elbows on the table. "You're going to get yourself killed, Carter."

"Then why are you here?" she asked, not looking up.

"Because someone has to make sure you don't drag the rest of us down with you," he shot back, though there was a faint softness in his tone.

"I'm not dragging anyone," Isabella said firmly, gathering the papers into a neat stack.

"You think you can take them on alone?" Ben asked, his voice rising slightly. "Because if you do, you're delusional."

"I'm not alone," she said, finally meeting his gaze. "I have you. And Rachel. And maybe even Adam, if he ever trusts me again."

Ben shook his head, his frustration evident. "Trust isn't enough. The Syndicate doesn't lose, Isabella. They've built this system to be untouchable."

"Every system has a flaw," she countered. "You just have to know where to look."

"And what if you can't find it?" Ben asked.

"Then I'll create one," Isabella said, her voice steady.

Ben sighed, leaning back in his chair. "You're impossible."

"Maybe," she said, a faint smile tugging at her lips.

He watched her for a moment, then stood. "Just... be careful. I mean it."

"I will," Isabella promised, though the weight of her words felt heavier than ever.

As Ben walked away, she turned back to her papers, her resolve hardening. This wasn't just about survival anymore—it was about taking back control. Her rebellion would be slow, quiet, and calculated. And it would start with finding the one thread that could unravel everything.

Chapter 14
The Web Tightens

The common room was unusually quiet, the usual hum of conversation replaced by whispers and furtive glances. Isabella stepped inside, sensing the tension immediately. Students huddled in small groups, their voices barely audible over the crackle of the old fireplace. She scanned the room, her stomach twisting as she caught snippets of hushed conversations.

"Did you hear?"

"I knew something like this would happen."

"They're saying he broke the rules. What did he think would happen?"

Isabella's heart pounded as she approached one of the groups. Rachel was there, her face pale and her arms crossed tightly over her chest.

"What's going on?" Isabella asked, her voice low.

Rachel flinched at the sound of her voice, then turned to face her. "You haven't heard?"

"Heard what?" Isabella demanded, her pulse quickening.

Rachel leaned closer, her voice dropping to a near whisper. "Evan. He's gone."

"Gone?" Isabella repeated, her brows furrowing.

"Expelled," Rachel said, her tone clipped. "He broke one of their rules. At least, that's what they're saying."

"What rule?" Isabella asked, her voice sharper now.

Rachel shook her head, glancing nervously around the room. "I don't know. Nobody does. All I know is they came for him last night. Packed up his things, cleared out his dorm. It's like he was never here."

Isabella's chest tightened, and she forced herself to keep her voice steady. "Did anyone see it happen?"

"No one's talking," Rachel said, her eyes darting to the others in the room. "But we all know what it means."

"What does it mean?" Isabella pressed, though she already felt the answer clawing at her mind.

"It means the Syndicate isn't playing games anymore," Rachel said, her voice trembling. "If they think you've stepped out of line, they'll make sure everyone knows what happens next."

Isabella clenched her fists, her mind racing. "This doesn't make sense. Evan was careful. He never did anything to draw attention to himself."

"Maybe he wasn't careful enough," Rachel whispered. "Or maybe they just wanted to send a message."

"Message received," muttered another student nearby, his voice laced with bitterness.

Isabella turned toward him. "What do you mean?"

He shrugged, his eyes fixed on the floor. "It's obvious, isn't it? They want us scared. They want us to know that no matter how careful we are, they're always watching."

The room fell into a tense silence, the weight of his words settling heavily over the group. Isabella's thoughts churned, her paranoia growing with each passing second. If the Syndicate could make someone like Evan disappear without warning, what chance did she have?

Rachel reached out, gripping Isabella's arm. "You see why I've been telling you to stop? This isn't a game, Isabella. They're not just watching—they're acting. And if you keep pushing, you'll be next."

Isabella pulled her arm free, her jaw tightening. "I can't just sit back and do nothing."

"Then at least be smart about it," Rachel hissed. "Because whatever Evan did, it wasn't enough to protect him. And it won't be enough to protect you either."

"I don't need protection," Isabella said, though the words felt hollow even as she spoke them.

Rachel stared at her, her eyes filled with a mix of fear and frustration. "You don't get it, do you? They don't need a reason. They just need an excuse."

The room buzzed with low murmurs again as the conversation shifted elsewhere, but Isabella couldn't focus. Her mind was already spinning, replaying every interaction she'd had with the Syndicate, every step she'd taken that might have caught their attention.

Her breath hitched as she realized just how precarious her position had become. The Syndicate wasn't just a shadowy presence anymore—it was a force, real and dangerous, and closer than she'd ever imagined.

As she turned to leave the common room, Rachel's voice stopped her.

"Promise me you'll be careful," Rachel said quietly, her voice barely audible over the crackle of the fire.

Isabella paused, her back to her friend. "I'll try."

But as she stepped out into the cold night air, she knew trying might not be enough. The Syndicate had made its move, and the stakes had never been higher.

Isabella sat across from Professor Thorne in his dimly lit office, the faint scent of old leather and polished wood lingering in the air. His desk, meticulously organized, was devoid of any personal touches—just stacks of papers and a single pen perfectly aligned with the edge. Thorne himself sat behind it, his hands folded neatly, his piercing eyes fixed on her like a hawk assessing its prey.

"You've been diligent," Thorne began, his voice smooth but unnervingly cold. "Your reports have been... thorough."

"Thank you," Isabella said cautiously, her stomach twisting. She kept her hands folded tightly in her lap to hide their trembling.

Thorne tilted his head slightly, a faint smile playing at his lips. "Loyalty is a trait we value highly at Barrington. It's what separates those who thrive here from those who... falter."

Isabella swallowed hard, the image of Evan's empty dorm flashing through her mind. "I understand."

"Do you?" Thorne leaned forward, his sharp gaze narrowing. "Because loyalty isn't just about following instructions. It's about intent. It's about proving, time and again, that you can be trusted implicitly."

"I've done everything you've asked," Isabella said, keeping her voice steady despite the knot tightening in her chest.

"Indeed," Thorne said, his smile sharpening. "But it's not just what you do that matters—it's why you do it. True loyalty comes from belief in the system, in its purpose. Tell me, Isabella, do you believe in what we do here?"

Her pulse quickened, but she forced herself to stay calm. "I believe in the opportunities Barrington provides. I believe in doing my best."

"A diplomatic answer," Thorne said, his tone laced with amusement. "But diplomacy only gets you so far."

"What do you want me to say?" Isabella asked, her voice firmer now.

Thorne leaned back in his chair, his fingers steepled as he studied her. "I want you to understand the importance of what we do. The Syndicate is not just an institution—it is a network, a foundation for success. It has shaped the brightest minds, the most influential leaders. But that kind of power requires discipline, order... and loyalty."

"I understand," Isabella said again, though the words felt hollow in her mouth.

"Good," Thorne said, though his tone suggested otherwise. He picked up the single pen on his desk and twirled it absently between his fingers. "Because loyalty, Miss Carter, is not a choice—it is a requirement. Those who fail to meet that requirement often find themselves... misplaced."

Her breath hitched at the thinly veiled threat. "I don't intend to fail."

"See that you don't," Thorne said, setting the pen down with a soft click. "Because loyalty is not just about surviving—it's about thriving. Those who embrace it find themselves rewarded. Those who resist…" He let the sentence hang, his smile widening ever so slightly.

Isabella clenched her fists beneath the desk, her nails digging into her palms. "I appreciate the guidance," she said, keeping her tone measured.

"I'm sure you do," Thorne said, his voice dripping with condescension. "But appreciation is not enough. Actions, Miss Carter, speak louder than gratitude. And your actions, while commendable, must continue to align with our expectations."

"I understand," Isabella said for the third time, though her stomach churned with every word.

"Do you?" Thorne asked, his gaze boring into hers. "Because loyalty is not just about obedience—it's about conviction. And conviction, Miss Carter, is not something one can fake."

The silence that followed was suffocating, and Isabella fought to keep her composure. Finally, Thorne leaned back again, a faint look of satisfaction crossing his face.

"That will be all for now," he said, dismissing her with a wave of his hand.

Isabella stood, her legs unsteady beneath her. As she turned to leave, Thorne's voice stopped her.

"One more thing," he said, his tone lighter but no less chilling. "You've done well so far, Miss Carter. But remember—loyalty is an ongoing process. There is no room for hesitation or doubt. Not here."

She nodded, her back still to him. "I'll remember."

"See that you do," Thorne said, his words following her out the door like a shadow.

As the heavy door clicked shut behind her, Isabella exhaled shakily, her heart pounding in her chest. Thorne's praise had felt more like a warning, a reminder that she was constantly under scrutiny. Every word, every action, every choice was being weighed, and one misstep could cost her everything.

Her paranoia deepened, but so did her resolve. If Thorne thought he could manipulate her into submission, he was wrong. She wouldn't let them win—not without a fight.

The library was nearly empty, the faint hum of the overhead lights blending with the soft rustle of pages being turned somewhere in the distance. Isabella sat at the farthest corner table, her mind still reeling from her conversation with Thorne earlier that day. The words loyalty and conviction echoed in her head like a relentless drumbeat.

She barely noticed Ben approach until he dropped into the chair across from her, sliding a USB drive across the table.

"What's this?" she asked, glancing up at him.

"Something you need to see," he said, his tone low. His usual smirk was absent, replaced by a grim expression that made her stomach tighten.

Isabella hesitated, her fingers hovering over the USB. "What's on it?"

"Proof," Ben said simply. "Of what we're up against."

She glanced around the library before picking up the drive and plugging it into her laptop. The screen flickered as a folder labeled **Encrypted Archives** popped up. Isabella's fingers hovered over the trackpad.

"How did you get this?" she asked, her voice cautious.

"Does it matter?" Ben said, leaning forward. "Just open it."

She double-clicked the folder, and her screen filled with documents, spreadsheets, and video files. Her pulse quickened as she clicked on the first document. It was a detailed report, its contents describing a scholarship student who had been closely monitored for months before their abrupt dismissal.

"This is..." Isabella began, but her voice trailed off as she scrolled further.

The file included timestamps of surveillance footage, excerpts of personal emails, and even transcripts of private conversations. It was invasive and chilling, laying bare the extent of the Syndicate's control.

"Keep going," Ben urged, his voice tight.

Isabella opened another file, this one detailing a faculty member's forced resignation. The report painted a picture of calculated pressure—rumors strategically leaked, their credibility questioned, until they had no choice but to leave.

"This is how they operate," Ben said, his voice breaking the silence. "They don't just control; they dismantle. Piece by piece, until there's nothing left."

Her chest tightened as she clicked on a video file. The grainy footage showed a young man sitting alone in what appeared to be a dorm room. Evan. He was speaking to someone offscreen, his voice barely audible over the static.

"I can't do this anymore," he was saying. "I thought I could handle it, but they're everywhere. They know everything."

The screen went dark. Isabella sat frozen, her hand still hovering over the trackpad.

"What happened to him?" she asked, her voice barely above a whisper.

"They made him disappear," Ben said bluntly. "And not just from Barrington. It's like he never existed. No records, no trail. Nothing."

Isabella leaned back, her mind racing. "How many people have they done this to?"

"Too many," Ben replied, his tone grim. "Students, faculty, even alumni. Anyone who steps out of line or asks too many questions."

She stared at the screen, the weight of the files pressing down on her. This wasn't just about her or the students who were still at Barrington. The Syndicate's reach extended far beyond what she'd imagined.

"They don't just control Barrington," she said, her voice shaking. "They control everything."

Ben nodded. "Now you see why this isn't just about surviving, Carter. If we don't push back, they'll keep expanding. And no one will be safe."

"But how do we fight something like this?" she asked, her voice laced with desperation. "They have everything—money, power, influence."

"We start small," Ben said, his tone steady. "We find cracks in their system and exploit them. We gather evidence, real evidence, and we get it into the right hands."

"And if there are no cracks?" Isabella asked, her gaze fixed on the screen.

Ben's expression darkened, but his voice remained firm. "Then we make some."

The silence that followed was heavy, the enormity of the situation settling over them like a dark cloud. Isabella looked at the USB drive, its small size a stark contrast to the massive implications of its contents.

The Syndicate wasn't just an oppressive force—it was a machine, methodical and unrelenting. And for the first time, Isabella realized the full extent of what she was up against.

She closed the laptop and looked at Ben, her resolve hardening. "We'll need more than this."

"Then we'd better get started," he said, his tone determined.

As they left the library together, the weight of the files lingered in her mind. The Syndicate's power was vast, but for the first time, she felt a flicker of hope. Small, but enough to push her forward.

There was no turning back now.

The afternoon light streaming through the tall windows of the administrative wing seemed muted, almost suffocating. Isabella sat stiffly in the chair outside Thorne's office, her hands folded tightly in her lap. Across from her, a small plaque on a desk read **Ms. Eliza Morgan, Executive Assistant**. Ms. Morgan herself sat behind it, her sharp features softened only by the faintest smile that didn't quite reach her eyes.

"You're early," Ms. Morgan said, glancing up from her tablet.

"I didn't want to keep Professor Thorne waiting," Isabella replied, her tone measured.

"Good instincts," Ms. Morgan said, her smile widening slightly. She set the tablet down and leaned forward, her piercing gaze locking onto Isabella's. "Thorne appreciates punctuality. He also appreciates... loyalty."

Isabella's stomach tightened. "I'm aware."

"Are you?" Ms. Morgan asked, her tone casual, though her eyes remained fixed on Isabella. "Because loyalty isn't just about showing up on time. It's about knowing your place, understanding your responsibilities, and following through without question."

Isabella forced a polite smile, though her chest felt like it was caving in. "I do my best to meet those expectations."

Ms. Morgan tilted her head, studying her. "Your best is a good start. But Thorne expects more. The Syndicate expects more. You understand that, don't you?"

"Yes," Isabella said, her voice steady despite the unease creeping through her.

Ms. Morgan leaned back in her chair, her hands resting lightly on the desk. "Good. Because students who fail to meet those expectations often find themselves... redirected."

"Redirected?" Isabella repeated, her pulse quickening.

"It's a polite term for removed," Ms. Morgan said, her smile sharpening. "But I'm sure you have no reason to worry. You've been diligent, haven't you?"

"Yes," Isabella said quickly, her heart pounding.

"Excellent," Ms. Morgan said, standing and walking around the desk. She perched on its edge, her posture deceptively relaxed. "Because diligence is rewarded, Miss Carter. Just as disloyalty is... corrected."

The words hung in the air, their meaning clear. Isabella's mind raced as she fought to maintain her composure.

"I have no intention of being disloyal," Isabella said, her voice firm but not defiant.

"Of course not," Ms. Morgan said, her tone dripping with faux warmth. "You seem far too intelligent for that. But intelligence can be a double-edged sword. Sometimes it leads to curiosity, and curiosity... well, it can be dangerous."

"I understand the boundaries," Isabella said, her hands gripping the edge of her chair.

"I'm glad to hear that," Ms. Morgan said, straightening and smoothing her skirt. "Thorne has high hopes for you, Miss Carter. Don't let him down."

The door to Thorne's office opened suddenly, and the man himself appeared, his sharp gaze flicking between the two women. "Miss Carter, come in."

Isabella rose, her legs unsteady beneath her. "Thank you, Professor."

Ms. Morgan's smile remained fixed as she stepped aside, her eyes following Isabella as she entered the office.

The door closed behind her, sealing her in with Thorne, but Isabella's mind was still reeling from Ms. Morgan's thinly veiled threat. The assistant's words had been calm, measured, almost pleasant, but their implications were chilling.

As Thorne began speaking, Isabella found it difficult to focus. Ms. Morgan's voice echoed in her mind, her warning clear: The Syndicate demanded absolute loyalty, and any deviation would be met with swift and decisive consequences.

For the first time, Isabella truly understood the stakes. This wasn't just about survival—it was about retaining her autonomy, her sense of self, in the face of a force that sought to consume her completely.

Her fists clenched at her sides as Thorne's words washed over her. She nodded when necessary, spoke when prompted, but her thoughts were elsewhere. The Syndicate's control was suffocating, its reach terrifying, but it wasn't absolute.

She couldn't allow it to be absolute.

When she left Thorne's office later, her resolve had solidified. Ms. Morgan's threat hadn't cowed her—it had ignited a spark. She couldn't fight openly, not yet, but she could plan, calculate, and prepare. The Syndicate wanted loyalty, but she wouldn't give it freely.

Not when the cost was her freedom.

Chapter 15
The Crossroads of Conviction

Thorne's office was darker than usual, the heavy drapes drawn tight against the afternoon sun. The only light came from the desk lamp, its pale glow casting long shadows across the room. Isabella stood stiffly in front of Thorne's desk, her hands clasped behind her back, her heart pounding as she waited for him to speak.

"Miss Carter," Thorne began, his voice calm but carrying an edge that set her on edge. "You've proven yourself capable over the past few months."

"Thank you, Professor," Isabella said carefully, her tone neutral.

Thorne leaned back in his chair, steepling his fingers as he studied her. "But capability is only part of what we value at Barrington—and within the Syndicate. Loyalty, conviction, and a willingness to act when called upon... those are the true marks of success."

"I understand," Isabella replied, though her chest tightened with every word.

"I hope you do," Thorne said, leaning forward. "Because it's time for you to prove where your loyalties lie."

Isabella swallowed hard, her stomach twisting. "What do you mean?"

Thorne slid a folder across the desk toward her. "There is a situation that requires... discretion. A matter of significant importance to the Syndicate. You're uniquely positioned to handle it."

She hesitated before picking up the folder, her hands trembling slightly as she opened it. Inside were a series of documents and photographs, each one detailing a young man she recognized from campus—Adam Sinclair.

"What is this?" she asked, her voice barely above a whisper.

"Adam Sinclair is a valuable asset," Thorne said, his tone measured. "But he's also a potential liability. His recent behavior has raised concerns within the Syndicate. We need to ensure his continued cooperation."

Isabella's throat tightened as she flipped through the pages, her eyes scanning the details. The task was clear: monitor Adam, gain his trust, and report any signs of dissent.

"You want me to spy on him," she said, the words tasting bitter in her mouth.

Thorne raised an eyebrow. "I want you to protect the integrity of this institution. Call it what you will."

Her hands clenched around the folder. "And if I refuse?"

Thorne's smile didn't reach his eyes. "Refusal is not an option, Miss Carter. This is a pivotal moment for you—a test of your loyalty and your commitment to the Syndicate's vision."

Isabella's mind raced, the weight of his words pressing down on her. "Why me?" she asked, trying to buy time.

"You're close to him," Thorne said simply. "He trusts you. That trust is an asset we cannot afford to waste."

"I don't know if I can do this," Isabella admitted, her voice trembling.

"You can," Thorne said, his tone firm. "And you will. Because the consequences of failure, Miss Carter, are not something you want to consider."

Her breath caught, the unspoken threat hanging heavy in the air. She glanced down at the folder again, her vision blurring as fear and guilt twisted inside her.

"You have until the end of the week to provide your first report," Thorne continued, his tone as calm as if he were assigning a routine essay. "I trust you'll make the right decision."

Isabella's head shot up, her eyes narrowing. "And if I don't?"

Thorne's smile returned, colder this time. "Then I would suggest reevaluating your priorities, Miss Carter. This is not a game. The Syndicate's work is critical, and your role in it is non-negotiable."

She stared at him, her fists tightening around the folder. Every instinct screamed at her to say no, to push back, but the reality of her situation left her feeling cornered. Refusal wasn't just a risk—it was a death sentence, one way or another.

"I understand," she said finally, her voice barely audible.

Thorne nodded, satisfaction flickering in his expression. "Good. I knew you'd see reason."

As she left the office, the folder clutched tightly in her hands, Isabella's mind was a storm of conflicting emotions. Thorne's ultimatum had left her no room to maneuver, no room to breathe. The Syndicate's control was absolute, and she was just another cog in its unrelenting machine.

But as she walked back to her dorm, her resolve began to harden. She might be trapped, but she wasn't powerless. If Thorne wanted her loyalty, he would have to earn it—and the Syndicate would have to work harder than ever to keep her in line.

For now, she would play their game. But she wouldn't play it by their rules.

The library was nearly deserted, the faint glow of the overhead lights casting long shadows across the tables. Isabella sat in their usual spot near the back, her thoughts tangled and heavy as she stared at the unopened folder on the table in front of her. Thorne's words echoed in her mind, their weight pressing down like a vice.

"I figured I'd find you here."

Ben's voice broke the silence, pulling her from her thoughts. She looked up as he slid into the seat across from her, his expression more serious than usual.

"Not in the mood, Ben," Isabella muttered, turning her gaze back to the folder.

"Good, because I'm not here to mess around," Ben said, leaning forward. "We need to talk."

"About what?" she asked, though she already had an idea.

Ben glanced around, lowering his voice. "About the Syndicate. And about getting out from under their thumb."

Isabella stiffened. "What are you talking about?"

"You know exactly what I'm talking about," Ben said, his tone sharp. "You've seen what they're capable of. You've felt it. And if you don't do something, they'll keep squeezing until there's nothing left of you."

"Keep your voice down," Isabella hissed, glancing around to ensure they were still alone.

Ben's voice dropped to a whisper, but his intensity didn't waver. "I'm serious, Carter. There's a group—students, a few alumni, even some faculty. They've been working in secret to fight back, to expose the Syndicate for what it really is."

Her chest tightened. "And you're part of this group?"

"Yeah," he admitted, leaning closer. "And you should be too."

Isabella shook her head, her hands gripping the edge of the table. "You don't know what you're asking."

"I know exactly what I'm asking," Ben said, his voice firm. "You think you're the only one who's scared? We all are. But if we don't stand up to them, who will?"

"They'll destroy us," Isabella said, her voice trembling. "You've seen what they do to people who cross them."

"They destroy people because they can," Ben countered. "Because no one's ever pushed back hard enough to stop them."

"And what happens when they find out about this... resistance?" she asked, her heart pounding. "What happens when they come for you?"

Ben's jaw tightened, but he didn't look away. "Then we make it count. Every move we make, every piece of information we expose—it weakens them. It shows people that they're not invincible."

Isabella exhaled shakily, her mind racing. "Why me? Why now?"

"Because you're smart," Ben said. "Because you've already got one foot in the door. Thorne trusts you, or at least he thinks he does. That's leverage, Carter. And leverage is how we win."

She stared at him, torn between fear and the flicker of hope his words ignited. "What if I can't do it? What if I mess up?"

"Then you mess up," Ben said simply. "But at least you'll have tried. At least you'll have done something."

The silence stretched between them, heavy and suffocating. Isabella glanced at the folder on the table, the weight of Thorne's ultimatum pressing against the lure of Ben's offer.

"I don't know if I can," she admitted, her voice barely above a whisper.

Ben reached across the table, his hand brushing hers. "You can," he said softly. "And you don't have to do it alone."

She looked up at him, searching his face for reassurance. "This isn't just about me, Ben. If I join you, if I get caught... it'll put everyone at risk."

"It's a risk we're willing to take," Ben said firmly. "Because doing nothing is worse."

Her throat tightened as she considered his words. The resistance was a chance—a dangerous, uncertain chance—but it was more than she'd had before.

"I need time," she said finally, pulling her hand away.

Ben nodded, though disappointment flickered in his eyes. "Take all the time you want, Carter. Just don't wait too long."

As he stood and walked away, Isabella sat in silence, her gaze shifting between the folder and the empty seat across from her. Thorne's demand had left her feeling trapped, but Ben's offer was a reminder that she wasn't powerless.

The question wasn't whether she could fight back—it was whether she was ready to risk everything to do it.

The wind outside rattled the windows of the dormitory, a low howl echoing through the narrow halls. In Rachel's room, the atmosphere was equally tense. Isabella stood by the window, her arms crossed as she stared out at the stormy night. Behind her, Rachel paced in tight circles, her movements jerky and anxious.

"You can't seriously be thinking about this," Rachel said, her voice sharp with panic.

"I haven't decided anything yet," Isabella replied, her tone calm but strained.

Rachel stopped pacing and turned to face her, her eyes wide and pleading. "Then don't. Don't even think about it. You know what happens to people who try to fight back. Look at Evan. Look at all the others. They disappear, Isabella. Gone, like they never existed."

Isabella turned to face her friend, her chest tightening. "And if we do nothing? What happens then? They keep taking and controlling and crushing anyone who steps out of line."

"At least we survive," Rachel said, her voice trembling. "Isn't that enough?"

"Is it?" Isabella asked, stepping closer. "Because it doesn't feel like surviving to me. It feels like suffocating."

Rachel's hands curled into fists, her frustration boiling over. "You don't understand, Isabella. You've only been here a few months. You don't know how deep their roots go, how far they're willing to go to protect themselves."

"Then tell me," Isabella challenged. "Help me understand."

Rachel hesitated, her gaze darting toward the door as if the walls themselves might be listening. She lowered her voice to a whisper. "The Syndicate isn't just a group of powerful people pulling strings behind the scenes. They're everywhere. They have connections in every corner of this campus, this city, and beyond. If you think you can outsmart them, you're wrong."

"I'm not trying to outsmart them," Isabella said, her voice soft but firm. "I'm trying to stop them."

Rachel's eyes filled with tears, and she shook her head. "You'll fail. And when you do, they won't just come for you—they'll come for anyone close to you. Me. Ben. Adam. Do you want that on your conscience?"

Isabella's breath hitched, the weight of Rachel's words pressing down on her. "I don't want to hurt anyone," she said, her voice breaking.

"Then don't," Rachel said, her tone almost desperate. "Stay quiet, keep your head down, and get through this. That's the only way to survive."

A knock at the door made both of them jump. Rachel quickly wiped her face and composed herself as Ben stepped into the room, his expression grim.

"Am I interrupting?" he asked, glancing between them.

"No," Rachel said sharply, crossing her arms. "We were just discussing how stupid this idea of yours is."

Ben raised an eyebrow. "I take it you've told her to stay in line, keep quiet, and let the Syndicate walk all over her?"

"Yes," Rachel snapped. "Because it's the only way to stay alive."

"And that's enough for you?" Ben shot back, his tone cutting.

"It's better than getting killed," Rachel retorted, her voice rising.

Isabella stepped between them, her head pounding. "Stop. Both of you."

They fell silent, their anger still simmering as they stared at each other. Isabella turned to Ben first.

"Rachel's right," she said, her voice measured. "This is dangerous. And if we're not careful, we'll all pay the price."

Ben's jaw tightened, but he said nothing.

Then she turned to Rachel. "But he's right too. If we don't fight back, we're just letting them win. I can't live like that, Rachel. I won't."

Rachel's eyes filled with tears again, but this time she didn't argue. Instead, she sat down heavily on the edge of her bed, her hands shaking.

"I'm scared for you," she admitted, her voice barely above a whisper. "I'm scared for all of us."

"I know," Isabella said, her own voice breaking. "But I have to do something. I can't just sit back and watch this happen."

The room fell into an uneasy silence, the tension thick enough to cut. Ben stepped forward, his tone softer now. "You don't have to make a decision right this second. But when you do, we'll figure it out together."

Isabella nodded, her gaze shifting between her two closest allies. "I'll think about it," she said, though her resolve was already forming.

Rachel looked up at her, her expression a mix of fear and resignation. "Just promise me one thing," she said.

"What?"

"Be careful," Rachel whispered. "Please."

"I will," Isabella said, though she wasn't sure if she believed it herself.

As the storm outside raged on, the three of them sat in silence, each lost in their own thoughts. The Syndicate's power loomed large, but for the first time, Isabella felt the faintest flicker of hope. It wasn't much—but it was enough to keep her moving forward.

The crisp night air filled the library alcove, carried through a cracked window that Isabella had insisted they leave open. She sat at the table, staring at the folder Thorne had given her, its edges worn from her nervous hands. Across from her, Ben leaned back in his chair, his expression a mix of frustration and resolve.

"So," Ben began, breaking the silence. "What's the plan?"

Isabella didn't answer immediately, her fingers tracing the edge of the folder. Her mind churned, the weight of Thorne's ultimatum pressing against Ben's insistence that they fight back.

"I don't know," she admitted finally.

Ben sat forward, his elbows resting on the table. "That's not good enough, Carter. You can't just sit here and hope this works itself out."

"I'm not hoping for anything," Isabella shot back, her voice sharp. "I'm trying to figure out how to stay alive."

"And?" Ben prompted, his gaze steady.

"And," Isabella said, exhaling slowly, "I think... I think I have to play along. For now."

Ben's jaw tightened, but he didn't interrupt.

"If I push back too hard, if I refuse outright, Thorne will know," she continued. "And if he knows, it's over. For me, for you, for everyone."

"So you're going to do what he says?" Ben asked, his tone laced with disbelief.

"I'm going to make him think I am," Isabella clarified, meeting his gaze. "I'll give him just enough to keep him satisfied while we figure out our next move."

"And you're sure you can pull that off?" Ben asked, leaning closer.

"No," Isabella admitted, her voice trembling slightly. "But I don't see another choice."

Ben sighed, running a hand through his hair. "This is dangerous, Carter. If he even suspects you're not fully on board—"

"I know," she said, cutting him off. "But what other option do I have? Refuse him and get expelled? Or worse?"

"Working with him feels like giving up," Ben said, his voice low.

"It's not giving up," Isabella insisted. "It's buying time. Time for us to gather more information, time to figure out how to fight back."

Ben studied her, his expression softening slightly. "You're sure about this?"

"No," she said again, her voice barely above a whisper. "But I'm not ready to give up yet."

The room fell silent, the only sound the faint rustle of the wind through the open window. Isabella's thoughts churned as she weighed the risks of her decision. Playing along with Thorne felt like walking a tightrope over a pit of fire, but it was the only way she could see to stay in the game.

"Fine," Ben said finally, his tone reluctant. "But if we're doing this, you're not doing it alone. I'll help you."

She looked at him, her chest tightening with a mix of gratitude and guilt. "Thank you."

"Don't thank me yet," Ben said, leaning back again. "You haven't seen how bad I am at staying subtle."

Despite herself, Isabella let out a small laugh, the tension easing slightly. "We'll figure it out."

"You'd better hope so," Ben said, though his tone was lighter now. "Because if this goes south, we're both in trouble."

Isabella nodded, her resolve hardening. "It won't go south. Not if we're careful."

As the clock in the corner struck midnight, Isabella closed the folder and stood, slipping it into her bag. "I should go. Thorne expects me in his office first thing tomorrow."

Ben rose as well, his expression serious again. "Be careful, Carter. And remember—you're not alone in this."

"I know," she said, offering him a faint smile.

As she stepped out into the cold night air, the gravity of her decision settled over her. The path she'd chosen was fraught with danger, but it was the only way forward.

Isabella tightened her grip on the strap of her bag, steeling herself. If she was going to play Thorne's game, she'd have to play it better than he expected.

Her rebellion would be quiet, calculated, and relentless. She would play the loyal student while working with Ben to dismantle the Syndicate's control from within.

And no matter what, she wouldn't let them win.

Epilogue
A Whisper of Freedom

The campus of Barrington College stood silent under the silver light of a full moon. Shadows stretched across the cobblestone paths, their edges sharp and deliberate, as if even they conspired to conceal secrets. Isabella Carter stood at the edge of the Sundial Courtyard, clutching a folded letter in her trembling hands. The words scrawled across the expensive paper were succinct, almost clinical, but their meaning had shaken her to her core.

"You are closer than you think, but tread carefully. They are watching."

The signature at the bottom—a simple "B"—left little doubt in her mind. Ben had sent this, but why? Why now? They hadn't spoken in weeks, not since the moment in the library when he'd all but confirmed her worst suspicions. The Syndicate's grip wasn't just a theory—it was a reality, insidious and omnipresent.

Her gaze lifted to the spires of the administration building, their darkened windows reflecting the pale glow of the moon. Somewhere inside, Thorne was undoubtedly working late, plotting his next move. Her hands tightened into fists. He thought he controlled her, that his carefully crafted games had left her pliable and compliant. He was wrong.

Isabella's journey to this moment had been shaped by countless decisions—each one a precarious step along a razor-thin path. She had played the dutiful student, feigned ignorance, and even reported on Adam Sinclair at Thorne's behest. But every task, every moment of compliance, had been carefully calculated. She gave just enough to keep them satisfied while collecting the fragments of truth that had been hidden from her.

Her scholarship wasn't an opportunity. It was a contract, an unspoken agreement that bound her to the Syndicate's control. The whispers in the library, Rachel's desperate warnings, Ben's guarded revelations—they had all pointed to the same chilling reality: Barrington wasn't a college; it was a breeding ground.

Rachel had disappeared three days ago. At first, Isabella thought she'd gone home for a family emergency, but when her roommate's belongings were quietly removed by campus staff, the truth became impossible to ignore. Rachel had been taken. For what? For asking too many questions? For being too close to Isabella?

The guilt clawed at her, but it also solidified her resolve. Rachel had been right to fear the Syndicate, but Isabella couldn't follow her friend's advice to stay silent. The stakes were too high, and the consequences of inaction too dire.

"You can't seriously be thinking about this." Ben's voice broke the silence, pulling her from her thoughts. He emerged from the shadows of the courtyard, his expression grim.

Isabella turned to face him, the letter still clutched in her hand. "You sent this."

Ben nodded, his gaze flickering toward the administration building. "You're in deeper than I ever wanted you to be."

"You knew what this place was from the start," she said, her tone accusatory. "Why didn't you tell me?"

"Because knowing wouldn't have saved you," Ben replied. "It would've just made you a target sooner."

"I'm already a target," she said bitterly. "Rachel's gone. And I'm next, aren't I?"

Ben didn't answer immediately. His silence spoke volumes. "They won't stop until they have what they want. But you still have a choice."

"No, I don't," Isabella said, stepping closer. "Not anymore. The only choice I have is how this ends."

Ben studied her, his gray eyes searching hers. "You're planning something."

"Are you going to stop me?" she challenged.

He hesitated before shaking his head. "No. But I'm not going to save you either."

"I don't need saving," Isabella said, her voice firm. "I need you to trust me."

Ben's smirk was faint, almost sad. "You're a lot braver than I ever was."

Later that night, Isabella crept through the darkened halls of Barrington's main building, her heart pounding with every step. The envelope tucked into her jacket felt heavier than it should have, its contents a damning collection of documents she'd stolen from Thorne's office over the past month. They detailed the Syndicate's activities, its recruitment strategies, and the psychological profiling it used to select its "chosen scholars."

Her goal was simple: expose the Syndicate. But the risks were monumental. If she failed, there would be no second chance. The dim light of a laptop screen glowed in the far corner of the room she entered. Isabella slid the envelope into the outgoing mail slot, a calculated insurance policy should she not make it out. Then, she turned to the computer, her fingers flying across the keyboard as she uploaded the stolen files to a secure server. Every keystroke felt like a countdown.

The door creaked open behind her.

"Miss Carter." Thorne's voice was calm, almost amused. "I wondered how long it would take before you crossed the line."

Isabella's blood ran cold, but she forced herself to turn slowly. "You're too late, Professor. The truth is out."

Thorne stepped closer, his expression unreadable. "Do you really believe that? That you've won?"

"It's not about winning," Isabella said, her voice steady. "It's about making sure you lose."

Thorne's smile was thin, predatory. "You've underestimated the Syndicate, my dear. You may have lit a spark, but we have extinguished far greater flames."

"Then let's see if you can handle the fire," Isabella said.

The days that followed were a blur. Isabella's actions sent shockwaves through Barrington, and the fallout was swift. Faculty members resigned, students vanished, and whispers of the Syndicate's downfall spread like wildfire.

Isabella watched from the sidelines, her position tenuous. She wasn't safe, not yet. But for the first time, she felt the weight of the Syndicate's control begin to lift.

On a gray morning weeks later, Isabella stood at the campus gates, her duffle bag slung over her shoulder. Ben stood beside her, his hands in his pockets.

"You're leaving," he said, not a question but a statement.

"I have to," she replied. "If I stay, they'll find a way to silence me."

"And if they come after you?"

Isabella's gaze hardened. "Let them try."

Ben nodded, his smirk faint but genuine. "Good luck, Carter."

"You too," she said, turning away. As she walked down the cobblestone path, the weight of her choices settled over her.

She didn't know where the road ahead would lead, but for the first time, she felt free.

Behind her, Barrington loomed in the distance—a shadowed reminder of the secrets she'd uncovered and the battle she'd fought to expose them. The Syndicate wasn't gone, not completely, but its power had been shaken. And that was a start.